TALL TALES

ONCE UPON Another TIME

TALL TALES

JAMES RILEY

ALADDIN

NEW YORK   LONDON   TORONTO   SYDNEY   NEW DELHI

This book is a work of fiction. Any references to historical events, real people, or real places are used fictitiously. Other names, characters, places, and events are products of the author's imagination, and any resemblance to actual events or places or persons, living or dead, is entirely coincidental.

ALADDIN

An imprint of Simon & Schuster Children's Publishing Division
1230 Avenue of the Americas, New York, New York 10020
First Aladdin hardcover edition September 2022
Text copyright © 2022 by James Riley
Jacket illustration copyright © 2022 by Vivienne To
All rights reserved, including the right of reproduction in whole or in part in any form.
ALADDIN and related logo are registered trademarks of Simon & Schuster, Inc.
For information about special discounts for bulk purchases, please contact Simon & Schuster
Special Sales at 1-866-506-1949 or business@simonandschuster.com.
The Simon & Schuster Speakers Bureau can bring authors to your live event. For more
information or to book an event contact the Simon & Schuster Speakers Bureau
at 1-866-248-3049 or visit our website at www.simonspeakers.com.
Book designed by Laura Lyn DiSiena
The text of this book was set in Adobe Garamond Pro.
Manufactured in China 0522 SCP
2 4 6 8 10 9 7 5 3 1
Library of Congress Control Number 2022009773
ISBN 9781534425903 (hc)
ISBN 9781534425927 (ebook)

For anyone wishing upon a falling star:
Watch out, it might be an asteroid coming to
destroy the world! AAAAAAAAAH!

CHAPTER 1

nce upon a time, Lena the Giant would never have imagined having an audience of her own kind as she fought her way through a patrol of Faceless, the Golden King's mind-controlled army. But everything was different now, after she'd received her epithet from the Sparktender, and the other giants had seen her for who she really was: a five-and-a-half-foot tall giant, just like the rest of them in every way but height.

"Rip 'em up!" her father shouted, his voice a bit muffled by a bubble of thinner air, to keep him from getting air sickness down on the ground. "That's my girl!"

The visit had started as a test of the new magical bubbles, only to be interrupted by a Faceless patrol. Fortunately, her guests had been more than happy to wait as Lena took out the

Golden King's soldiers. Her father in particular had offered to help, but Lena had refused, not wanting to share.

A Faceless in a full suit of black armor swung its magical sword at Lena, and she ducked beneath it, then kicked out, knocking the Faceless into a tree. It slid down the trunk, then lit up with small bursts of light as the brainwashed Lilliputians inside all teleported away.

"Aw, they're escaping!" Creel the Sparktender shouted.

Lena frowned, then pointed at the pile of Faceless armor she'd already accumulated. "I know, they're quick. But that's why I grab trophies whenever I can!"

"Just watch out for those swords of theirs!" her mother said, wincing as another Faceless drove his sword down, slamming it into the ground just inches from where Lena had been standing. "They'll take away your strength again!"

Her mother had a point: the last time Lena had actually been struck by one of their swords, she'd lost all of the giant power in her arms. Sure, it'd come back over the last few weeks, and she was finally feeling normal again, but that wasn't something she wanted to repeat.

At least for her, it'd just been strength. Half of the residents of the Cursed City had been hit as well, changing them back to their non-cursed forms, which almost none of them preferred. Just like her own power, though, the residents' magical curses had returned, and the entire city's population was back to normal. Or the Cursed City version of normal.

Except now the residents also knew Lena's secret, that she was actually just a very short giant, not the regular human they'd taken her for. At first they'd treated her with fear and paranoia, but after she'd helped save the city from the Golden King's army, they'd come around quickly.

"Behind you!" her father roared, almost knocking a few of the remaining Faceless off their feet with the power of his voice. Lena kicked back without looking and sent another Faceless flying into the woods.

"Lena," said Rufus, her horse-sized cat, as he trotted away from her mother's foot and settled himself down on the ground right in the middle of the battle, no longer afraid of the Faceless after fighting them with Lena so many times. "I am hungry. Treats?"

"Just a minute, little man," she said, punching another Faceless in the helmet, which went flying off. Without the protection of the headpiece, various tiny men and women inside quickly scrambled down farther into the armor, at which point several more bursts of light appeared as they teleported to safety.

These were Lilliputians, as small as giants were big, and the Last Knight's own people. For years they'd been infected by the Golden King's shadow magic, being forced to fight under his command. Fortunately, the Last Knight had used a magical item called the Cauldron of Truth on some captured Faceless to free their minds, and those Lilliputians had then returned to their homeland to help start a rebellion against the Golden King.

But there were far more Lilliputians still under the shadow's power than had been freed, and the king wouldn't let up until he destroyed the Cursed City. Unfortunately, without the Cauldron of Truth, all Lena could do was make sure these Faceless never got anywhere close. The city's protective spell had just about been restored, ensuring that no one with any bad intentions could even find the city. Mrs. Hubbard had spent countless hours the last few weeks working to get it back up, but the magic took time, and the city needed protecting.

And that's where Lena came in. After all, giants fight to show their might, as the saying went, and there was nothing Lena enjoyed more than getting to use her full strength to protect her friends and loved ones.

"Last one!" Creel shouted as a Faceless turned away from Lena to stalk Rufus. She gasped, the idea that her cat might be in danger sending her into a fury, and leapt forward with all her strength. Her giant power propelled her straight into the Faceless, and she slammed the armor's torso right off its legs.

"Get 'em!" her father shouted as brainwashed Lilliputians came pouring out of the armor, each one equipped with their own magical teleportation device. Lena knew that if she could just grab one, she could bring them to the Last Knight and free the Lilliputian's mind.

But even with Rufus joining in to hunt the tiny people, it was quickly apparent that they were both too slow, as the Lilliputians all disappeared, leaving behind that same burst of magical light. Lena growled in frustration, but she really couldn't complain. After all, the Cursed City was safe, another Faceless patrol had been wiped out, and she'd even gotten to show off a bit for her parents and Creel.

"Look at you go, Lena!" her father shouted, pulling out a nearby tree and shaking it in excitement. Her mother and Creel both began clapping, and all three giants grinned widely. The praise hit Lena almost like a giant punch, and she took a step back in surprise. This was just all so new and *wonderful*, not having to hide her true size from other giants, and even getting to flaunt her strength for them. It was like nothing she was used to, and she never wanted it to end.

But even the giants' magical air bubbles wouldn't last forever, and she didn't want her family or Creel to suffer from air sickness, which fogged up giants' brains to the point they lost all control, and might potentially put the Cursed City in danger. So while she could have listened to their applause for another few days, it was time for them to climb back up the mountain to the giant village in the clouds.

"I'm so glad you could all come down to visit!" she shouted up at them. Her mother pushed one of her fingers into the ground, and Lena threw her arms around the finger, hugging it tightly. "Promise you'll come back soon!"

"We certainly will, now that we can do it safely!" Creel said, tapping the air bubble around his head. "And please thank that witch who came up with these again. They're just fantastic."

"I will!" Lena promised, knowing she owed Mrs. Hubbard big-time, and not just for the bubbles. The owner of the Boot-ique, a Cursed City store built within a discarded giant boot, Mrs. Hubbard had openly welcomed Lena when she'd first visited. There was no one in town that Lena owed more to, and that debt just kept growing. "But you should all go back now before the thinner air starts running out in there."

"Love you, Lena girl," her father said, his voice a bit gravelly as he sniffed. He tried to wipe a tear away, only to smack his finger against the air bubble, so he looked away instead. "We're just so proud. So, so proud."

Lena had to look away herself, though she couldn't hide her own loud sniff. She rubbed the back of her hand against her now-wet eyes, then waved at her parents and Creel as they turned to clomp back toward the mountain that once Lena had descended to explore the human world below the clouds.

"Treats *now?*" Rufus said, bumping his head into her impatiently. At his size, he almost knocked her over with every headbutt.

"Let me just tie up all the armor, okay?" she said, moving to do just that. "If we leave it out in the open, another patrol might find it, and figure out they're close to the city."

Rufus's ears flattened in irritation, but he helped collect various pieces of armor using his teeth as Lena snaked a rope through it all. A few moments later, she stood back up with a satisfied sigh and surveyed the field of battle.

"Not too bad," she said, nodding. "Didn't even knock down

a tree this time. Other than that one Dad pulled up."

"Lena is the best," Rufus said through a mouthful of helmet. "Treats? Treats. Treats?"

She scratched behind his ears, then moved to grab the roped-together armor, happier than she'd ever been in her life. And the best part was, even with the threat of the Golden King out there, she knew that between herself, the Last Knight, and her genie friend Jin, they could handle it and keep everyone safe.

After all, with a genie on *their* side, what could possibly go wrong?

CHAPTER 2

This is all wrong!" Jin shouted at the translucent ghost woman standing in front of him. He pointed at the page of the *Half Upon a Time* Story Book he'd just read. "How did a fairy queen ever beat an *ifrit*, an elder genie?"

Jillian, the Cursed City's Invisible Cloud of Hate, just sighed. "You've been reading that book for what, weeks now? And you're still not done?"

"Hey, with writing this good, I want to enjoy it!" Jin said indignantly as the walls shook in his new home in the Cursed City, a loud reminder that Lena had visitors outside the city.

"'Writing this good'? This must be the only book you've ever read, I'm guessing?" Jill asked with a snort.

Jin narrowed his eyes. "Yes, and *you're* the one who wanted me to read it in the first place!"

"That's because those three Story Books explain all of *this*!" Jill shouted, waving her hand around.

Jin raised an eyebrow. "What, my house?" He glanced at the bed, table and chairs, and small kitchen in the house he'd subtly added to the list of Cursed City buildings that needed rebuilding. Okay, it hadn't exactly been destroyed in the fight against the giants like most of the rest of the city had, since it hadn't even existed at that point . . . but for all he'd done to help the city, Jin felt like he deserved a place to rest apart from the magical ring that granted its bearer three genie wishes.

"No, not this *place*, I meant everything with the Golden King and the Last Knight and all," Jill said, rubbing her forehead, which she seemed to do more and more often with him for some reason. Maybe she was itchy.

"I haven't seen either of *them* in the book so far," Jin said. "What I *have* seen is this random prince's fairy godmother fights a genie, and that's after one of her people trapped it in a magical mirror for years. Who are these fairy people, and why do they hate genies so much?"

Jill groaned. "Fairies? Really? We're going *that* basic? Okay, fine. How much do you already know?"

"Only the worst parts!" Jin shouted. "From what I was told,

the genie elders started this whole serve-humanity-with-wishes horribleness because an ifrit was out of control and almost destroyed this world. But if this book is right, that all only happened like ten *years* ago?"

"Twelve," Jill corrected.

"Which means I'm the first and *only* genie who's ever had to do this!" Jin continued to shout, floating in the air now, he was so upset. "I'd thought this was going on for thousands of years!"

What difference does it make when it started? asked the cosmic knowledge in Jin's head, the sum total of information contained within the known universe that Jin couldn't access directly, but instead was controlled by the horrible, evil, cruel voice in his mind. Apparently the genie elders thought he wasn't ready for omniscience yet. What did they know, though?

Um, everything, just like I do.

Including that I was the first *genie who had to go through this whole be-selfless trial?*

Of course, the cosmic knowledge said, its calmness making Jin even angrier. *What does that matter?*

Because it's wrong, *and no one should have to do it, especially me! But at least if other people had to go through it, then I wasn't alone or something.*

"Oh, it's definitely a scam all right," Jill said, answering the last thing he'd said out loud. "But is that all you know about fairies?"

"Well, now I know they're evil and hate genies, so what else do I need to know?"

Jill sighed. "They're not evil, Jin. Just the opposite. They tried to protect the world from the Wicked Queen, and anyone else who uses shadow magic. And not all fairies are like their queens. Most are tiny flying creatures you've probably seen around the Cursed City, with wings as big as their bodies. They look like little humans—"

"Not this fairy queen, Merriweather!" Jin said, tapping the page again. "She was taller than your brother. So what's *her* story?"

The ground shook again, and the new house creaked louder this time. Hopefully the Cursed City residents that Jin had ordered to work on his place had built it up to giant code. Now that Lena's parents could visit safely, this kind of shaking was going to get a lot more regular.

"I was getting to that!" Jill roared. "Regular fairies are small, but the fairy queens are the size of human adults, and no longer have wings. And Merriweather is the queen of the queens, basically." She tilted her head thoughtfully. "I've also heard there are fairy princesses, but who knows what *they* look like."

"Yeah, okay, but the prince in this book said this Merriweather was his godmother," Jin said. "So what, when they're not fighting shadow magic, the fairy queens just serve human royalty? Fancy rulers protecting their own kind at the expense of normal people?"

Jill started to respond, then paused. "Yeah, that part isn't great. But mostly, the fairy queens really *are* a powerful magical force for good—"

"Except when they're throwing ifrits in magic mirrors," Jin said, fuming. "I swear, if I ever find this Merriweather, I'm going to . . . well, probably run in the opposite direction, but not before giving her *such* a dirty look!"

"She wasn't the one who trapped that ifrit," Jill said, shaking her head. "The one you should be mad at was a rogue fairy queen named Mal—"

"Yeah, yeah, I read that part," Jin said, rolling his eyes. "Whatever. I think they're all terrible. Would have served them right if the ifrit *had* destroyed the world, maybe just for like a minute or two."

"Hey, I'm not saying it didn't deserve to be angry!" Jill shouted. "But put that anger into a hobby or something. Take up pottery, don't destroy the whole world! There are a lot of non-fairy queens who didn't trap anyone in mirrors here, if you hadn't noticed."

"Maybe I'll put this Merriweather in a magic mirror *herself*," Jin said, nodding. "See how she likes it."

Very original, the cosmic knowledge said.

Shouldn't you stick to facts, not opinions? Jin thought back.

Here's a fact: you're getting off track about the fairy queens. You were supposed to be reading about Sir Thomas, the Last Knight. Or do you not remember how you overheard his conversation with that Lilliputian Lena captured? How Thomas wants to take over the Golden King's shadow magic and use it himself?

Right, right, *that* whole thing. The cosmic knowledge did have a point. Lena's hero, Sir Thomas, was a Lilliputian, just like the Faceless, something Thomas had kept a secret from the Cursed City by wearing a human-sized suit of armor and operating it from the helmet. And that wasn't the only thing the Last Knight was hiding: he'd actually served the Wicked Queen years before, a tyrant with the power of shadow magic, just like the Golden King. Coincidence? Jin didn't buy it.

Maybe you'd know if it was coincidence or not if you finished the books, like Jill said, the cosmic knowledge pointed out.

Jin rolled his eyes. Hadn't he gotten enough of the story from Jill before even opening the book? And worse, Jill let it slip that Thomas didn't even show up until the third Story Book, *Once Upon the End*. So now he had to read *three* books just to find out more about Thomas?

That's traditionally the way to learn things, yes.

Or, hear me out, I could just lie and pretend I've read them, and then trick people into telling me what I need to know.

Oh, of course, what a classic. Let's see how often you've managed to pull that off. Checking now, I'm sure it's a long list . . . no, it's zero. Zero times. That was easy.

Jin growled quietly but didn't respond. None of this mattered anyway. He'd already told Lena what the Last Knight had said, how he wanted to use the Golden King's shadow magic himself, and she claimed it was probably for the good of everyone. Right, of course, because working for someone who *called* themself the Wicked Queen would definitely have the world's best interests at heart.

Okay, sure, this Wicked Queen person had apparently used shadow magic on all of Lilliput, taking over its people and forcing Thomas to serve her. But somehow Thomas had been freed and set out to save the rest of the Lilliputians from the shadow, only to have the Golden King take it over and use them as his Faceless army.

While it might make for a good story, what it *didn't* do was help Jin prove to Lena that the Last Knight was a bad guy. And even worse, she now seemed to trust *Jin* less, because she thought he was trying to turn her against Thomas! It was all basically a nightmare, considering how cute Lena was.

"I don't know why I'm even bothering with these books," Jin said to Jill. "Lena is convinced Sir Thomas is a big hero, no pun intended, and won't listen to whatever I have to say about him."

"So *show* her," Jill said, narrowing her eyes. "You've got magic. Take her back in time, so she can see him sending the world's greatest hero, i.e., *me*, to get turned into a golden statue. Or show her how he was cackling evilly about using the Golden King's shadow magic himself!"

He wasn't cackling evilly, the cosmic knowledge in Jin's head pointed out. *He didn't even laugh at all. Jill seems to be a bit biased.*

Yeah, well, who can blame her? Jin thought back. *She's right— he sent her and her family into a trap. And even if that was a mistake, the Last Knight wants to use that shadow to do . . . something. And until we know what, I don't trust him as far as I can throw him, which is miles, easily. In fact, the next time I see him, I'm going to demand he tell Lena the truth—*

His body began to tingle oddly, a familiar sensation that hadn't happened in a few months. The magical ring that controlled Jin was calling for him. Which meant—

Ah, the Last Knight is summoning you! the cosmic knowledge said. *Sounds like you're about to get your chance!*

CHAPTER 3

Lena dragged a dozen sets of empty Faceless armor down the main street of the Cursed City with Rufus at her side, proud of her latest fight. The noise from the armor clanking and clattering together brought the residents from their homes to see what was going on, and she beamed at them, hoping they felt even just a bit safer at the sight of it.

Mr. Ralph and the former chancellor Pinocchio, two of her closest friends in the city, turned onto the street, and she grinned even wider at them. "That's twelve more Faceless that won't be bothering us!" she said.

But both Mr. Ralph and the wooden puppet looked away, not responding.

Lena paused, not sure what had happened. "Everything

okay?" she said, and Mr. Ralph glanced over, nodded, then turned away again.

"Just busy, you know how it is," he said, his gingerbread hands crumbling slightly as he fiddled with them. "We should be going. Lots of damage to fix still."

Damage? Lena frowned, not sure what he was talking about. "I thought Jin got everything rebuilt already?"

"Oh, there's still some left over," Pinocchio said, his nose growing slightly. The puppet tried to push it back in but couldn't move it, so instead he just looked away. "Must be going now!"

And with that, he and Mr. Ralph quickly turned onto a side street.

Lena blinked, wondering what was going on. Several residents were giving her dark looks, as if she'd done something wrong. Had she?

Or was this about her parents' and Creed's visit somehow? They weren't the softest of walkers, so maybe the residents had gotten disturbed by the shaking?

"I'm sorry if my family was a bother!" she told one of the onlookers. "I'll make sure any visiting giants are quieter next time."

"Or you could make sure they stay up where they belong, in the clouds," said a man Lena didn't know, before a woman shushed him, and he turned away.

"Lena?" said a familiar voice, and Lena turned to find Mrs. Hubbard walking toward her, several of her children in tow. The sight of one of her oldest human friends was a relief, and Lena quickly dragged the Faceless armor over to her, just to find out what was going on.

"Treats Lady!" Rufus shouted, and bounded toward Mrs. Hubbard, who grinned and quickly pulled out some large fish treats for the cat. He grabbed them from her hand and began devouring them happily in the middle of the street, purring loudly.

"I'm so happy to see you, Mrs. Hubbard," Lena said, shaking her head. "Did something happen while I was gone? Everyone seems annoyed with me."

Mrs. Hubbard gave her a sad look. "I don't know if your giant friends realize their own strength, Lena. We had quite the shaking here in town, and I think it reminded people of . . . well, less happy times."

Mrs. Hubbard had caught herself before saying it, but Lena knew she was referring to the attack by the giant king. Denir and his guards had come searching for the Spark, a source of magic and healing for the giants that Lena had accidentally stolen, but was now returned.

"I'm so, so sorry!" she said, moving in closer. "I'll fix this, I promise. Next time they visit, I'll make sure they move as carefully as they can. This *won't* happen again."

Mrs. Hubbard sighed. "It might just be that the Cursed City isn't quite ready for more giant visits, Lena. After everything that happened in the attack, the other residents are all a bit . . . concerned. I've kept some of the louder naysayers quiet as much as I could, but . . ."

"But?" Lena said, a cold wave of fear passing through her.

"But they're demanding Pinocchio ban all giants from the ground," Mrs. Hubbard finished. "Not you, of course. They know you're one of the good ones, but—"

Lena almost choked. "One of the *good* ones? What is that supposed to mean?"

"Oof, Mom," said one of Mrs. Hubbard's children, and the woman seemed to realize she'd misspoken.

"I only meant that they know *you* would never hurt them, but don't yet know the same about the other giants," Mrs. Hubbard said, turning pink with embarrassment. "There are so many stories about giants eating humans that it's hard to come around so quickly, but even without that, we're still the size of mice to them. I'm not sure there's any amount of care they could take that would keep our city completely safe."

"Leave your kind where they belong," someone shouted from down the street, "up in the clouds, where they can't tear down our city!"

"You just bought yourself a ban from the Boot-ique, Roger!" Mrs. Hubbard shouted back at the passerby, who quickly panicked and took off running. "Don't listen to him," she said, turning back to Lena. "The city *will* get used to them, but it will take time, that's all. Maybe in a year or two—"

"A *year* or two?" Lena said, her eyes widening.

"Or you could just go visit them?" Mrs. Hubbard said, not looking happy about any of this. "I'm truly sorry, Lena. None of this is your fault, but this kind of thing is never easy. Think about how hard a time the goblins had after the Wicked Queen's war, when no one trusted them. Most kingdoms still won't allow them in."

Lena swallowed hard, having no idea what to say. She loved Mrs. Hubbard almost as a second mother, but after Lena had proved herself during the Golden King's attack, she'd figured everything was okay now between the residents and giants.

Apparently that wasn't even remotely the case. Homes could be rebuilt, but trust was something else entirely. "I appreciate you telling me, Mrs. Hubbard," Lena said numbly, not knowing what else to say. "I guess I'll talk to you later."

"Lena, wait!" Mrs. Hubbard said, but Lena moved quickly away, not sure she could hide how much this hurt for any longer. She knew Mrs. Hubbard would try to make things better, but there were no words to fix this, not with the city's residents afraid of Lena's people.

As Rufus raced to catch up to her, some strange twittering caught Lena's attention, and she looked up to find fairies on the rooftops above watching her. At least *they* didn't seem particularly annoyed at her, though for all she knew, they were gossiping about the giants as well.

As she continued toward Thomas's house, people on the street seemed to find any possible activity they could to avoid speaking to her. Some didn't even bother being subtle and turned down side streets or whirled around and walked the other direction.

Each clanking of the armor now made Lena even more anxious, not sure if it was contributing to how the residents were acting or not. Part of her wanted to drop it all in the street and run to the knight's house, but that'd just be making a mess that not many others in the city could handle, so she gritted her teeth against the noise and kept on.

All in all, her mood couldn't have fallen any further if she'd tumbled off the mountain leading back to her giant home in the clouds.

Fortunately, the knight's house wasn't *too* far, and she made it without running into any more of her friends, which seemed like a blessing at this point. But as she approached, she heard voices from inside, one clearly the Last Knight's, and the other one she'd never heard before, much more melodic than the knight's. Who was he talking to?

"Please, Thomas, you *must* listen to us," the new person said. "If you attempt this, the consequences could be catastrophic!"

"And if I don't, things will be worse," Lena heard Thomas say. "I respect your stories, but we don't know that this one is set in stone. I'm afraid I have to try, Merriweather."

"Then we will do as we must as well," this Merriweather said. A strange sort of humming sounded from within, and then Lena heard the Last Knight sigh and approach the door. She quickly moved away so he wouldn't know she had been listening, only for all the armor to clank loudly, completely giving her away. She cringed as the knight opened the door.

"Good, I'm glad you're here, Lena," he said, his helmet's visor down as always to hide the fact that he was a six-inch-tall Lilliputian, just like the Faceless. He glanced behind her. "That's *quite* a haul. Any of my people captured?"

Lena bit her lip. "Not since that first time. I didn't want to hurt any of them, so they were able to teleport with their little devices again. Sorry about that!"

He waved away her apology. "We unfortunately have far more concerning things to worry about now. I've just been warned that the Golden King's plan has come to fruition, and he's begun his attack." He let out a long breath, looking away. "He means to cover the entire world in shadow magic, Lena, just like what happened to Lilliput and the shadowlands. This whole city will fall under his control in a matter of *days*."

Lena's mouth dropped, and she had no idea what to say.

Fortunately, Rufus had his priorities straight. "Treats Lady is in danger?!" he shouted, his whiskers twitching. "Attack! Attack the Gold Man, and bite him a hundred times!"

CHAPTER 4

'm being summoned," Jin said to Jill, feeling the pull of a summoning from his ring. "Maybe Thomas knows that we're onto him?"

"Well, don't let him torture you until I get there!" Jill shouted as he started to disappear. "Not because I can help, but because I think it'd be kind of funny, honestly!"

"You know what *I* think would be funny?" Jin shouted back. "If the Last Knight took your sword and—"

"And what?" the Last Knight asked. Jin blinked, then cringed as he realized he'd already been transported to the knight's side, just outside the man's house in the Cursed City. He sighed deeply with embarrassment, then immediately brightened at the sight of Lena, back from the visit with her parents.

"Finally!" Jin said, not able to hide his excitement. He reached out and hugged her tightly, breathing in deeply the smell of metal and joy that was her distinguishing odor whenever she fought the Faceless.

Unfortunately, she returned the hug with a bit less enthusiasm. That was fair, given that Jin was probably about to be interrogated by the Last Knight, and Lena must have been torn between which of her two favorite people to believe.

Good to see you're concentrating on being more humble, the cosmic knowledge said.

Oh be quiet. I haven't seen her in weeks!

And if you want to ever see her again, I'd suggest not sniffing when you hug her.

. . . Fair.

"Jin, I was just visited by a fairy queen, and she alerted me to something terrible," the Last Knight told him, and suddenly all the jokes about being tortured felt a lot less funny.

"I know: they hate genies," Jin said quickly. "But that's obviously a horrible prejudice on their part, and we can all agree we shouldn't take anything they say seriously because of it."

Lena gave him an odd look. "What are you talking about? This isn't about you."

Her words hit hard, right in his gut, which was already filled with fear and coldness and probably the remains of lunch. *This isn't about me? What kind of horrible thing is* that *to say to a person?*

Maybe she just means that this isn't about you?

Now don't you start. Everything *should be about me!*

"The Golden King has begun to spread his shadow magic across the world, and we have just days before it reaches us," the knight said, his voice low and grim. "If we can't stop him, everyone in the Cursed City will fall under his power."

"Not to mention literally everyone else," Lena pointed out, fiddling with her hands nervously. "I don't even want to think about what would happen if it reached my village in the clouds!"

Jin blinked, slowly catching up. The fairy queen *hadn't* come to fight him, like she had the ifrit? And this was just about the Golden King, who couldn't even hurt Jin now that Thomas had Jin's ring? He let out a huge breath and grinned. "Well, that's not so bad!" Lena gave him a horrified glance, and he quickly threw up his hands in surrender. "I mean, it's not so bad, because it's *worse* than I thought. The absolute worst, in fact. So terrible!" He looked at the knight. "So, I guess you brought me here to help evacuate the city with a wish or two? Try to keep everyone ahead of the shadow magic?"

The knight shook his head. "That might buy us some time, so perhaps that makes sense for now. But it's only a temporary fix at best. To save our world, I must travel to Lilliput, gather what rebels we've freed so far, and together we'll take down the Golden King once and for all. It's the only way to stop his shadow magic."

Jin wrinkled his nose, not enjoying the lack of commitment to the wish. But the knight's words seemed to energize Lena. *"Yes!"* she shouted, and her giant, annoying cat Rufus began purring. "I've been waiting to do this for weeks. Let's go *get* him! Just give me a few minutes to get some weapons, and I'll be ready to go."

"Yeah, me too," Jin said quickly. "I'm ready to go right *now*, actually. So I'll be coming, just to keep everyone safe, you know, so no one gets hurt—"

The knight put a hand on Lena's shoulder. "I'm afraid I need you here, Lena. The Golden King might try to divide our attention us by throwing the Faceless against the Cursed City again. We can't take the chance that they'll find a way through the protective spell or take it down like the giants did."

Lena's mouth dropped open. "Wait, what? You're leaving me behind?"

"Yeah, *what*?" Jin said. "You're leaving us behind? What are you thinking?"

The knight slowly turned to look at him, and even with the helmet's visor down, Jin could feel the coolness from that look. "I'm thinking that I can't leave these people unprotected, young Jin."

"Hey!" shouted a voice from nearby, and Jin looked over his shoulder to find Jill walking over. "Next time you plan on disappearing, maybe tell me where you'll be reappearing first? I had to track you down by the sound of yelling!"

Before Jin could respond to Jill, Lena spoke first, not having been able to hear anything the ghostly woman said. "Jin can protect the city, and I can go with *you*," she said, practically begging the knight now, if also being incredibly rude about leaving Jin behind. "I can help—you *know* I can! I beat the Golden King once, and I can do it again. You might need me!"

"I would welcome your help without hesitation, in any other situation," the knight replied. "But I believe our only chance to beat the Golden King is through stealth. The Lilliputians I've freed from the shadow have been preparing for this. The king has locked himself in a human-sized castle just outside Lilliput, which my allies can sneak us into. With any luck, we'll be able to capture the human twins who control the magic itself, and free the rest of my people. At that point, we'll be able to bring the Golden King to justice, *finally*."

"And I can help with *all* of that!" Lena argued. "Even if I have to . . . get *small*. Rufus has a shrinking collar." She looked down at the ground and began picking at her fingernails. "It's not as bad as the growth ring. And if it's just temporary—"

The knight shook his head. "I know how hard that is for you to make that offer, Lena, and I can't tell you how much I appreciate it. But there's more." He paused. "I didn't want to mention this, as it's not your fault in any way, but . . . I can't have you around the shadow magic. It's too dangerous."

"Dangerous?" Lena said, looking back up at him with one eyebrow raised. "You mean if it takes control of me? That's the same danger you'll be in, and I can take care of myself!"

"No, that's not what I mean," the knight said, and coughed slightly. Now Jin was curious too. What was bothering him so much that he wouldn't take a girl with giant strength to a fight?

"Then what is it?" Lena asked.

"Uh-oh," Jill whispered. "Don't say it."

Jin raised an eyebrow. Don't say what?

"Shadow magic has been around for millennia," the knight

said, sounding even more uncomfortable now. "It seeps into the world whenever it's been freed, and as it does, it . . . changes things."

"Changes *what* things?" Jin asked, not able to stop himself, in spite of Jill's warning.

"Everything," the knight said. "The land, its people, anything it touches. And one of the things it changed was . . ." He briefly glanced at Lena, then looked away.

Lena's face went pale like the moon. "Giants?" she said, so quiet Jin could almost not hear her. "Shadow magic *changed* my people?"

The knight shook his head, and for a moment, Jin felt relieved. Lena was *not* going to take it well if the knight had said shadow magic was influencing her people!

"It didn't change them," he said sadly. "It *created* them."

CHAPTER 5

Lena just stood there, her mouth hanging open, having no idea what to say. Shadow magic had *created* the giants? It couldn't be true. There was no way.

Because if giants were somehow created by the shadow, that meant this evil, dark magic was the reason . . . that it was *part of* . . .

"No," she said finally, clenching her fists so tightly, her nails bit into her palms. "That's just some horrible rumor because no one down here trusts giants. We *weren't* created by evil magic; I don't care what you say!"

The knight slowly opened his visor, revealing his six-inch-tall self, and shook his head. "It's no rumor, Lena. This comes directly from the fairy queens, who have fought against the shadow their whole lives." He turned away, like he couldn't look her in the eye. "Your people moved to the clouds because they had to. The dark magic infected them, growing their human bodies until they couldn't live on the ground anymore, not without the air sickness poisoning their minds."

Her heart felt like it was in a vise, and for some reason, she couldn't take a full breath. Spots began popping in front of her eyes, and for a moment she thought she might faint, but Jin grabbed her arm, helping to support her. She started to pull her arm away but saw a look of actual concern on his face, and reluctantly left it.

"The fairy queens aren't necessarily right," Jin said quietly. "They hate my kind too, so maybe they're just terrible people."

"I'm *so* sorry, Lena," Thomas said, his voice muffled now as he closed his visor once more. "I didn't mean to tell you like this. To be honest, I *never* planned on telling you. I hoped it wouldn't matter."

"What wouldn't matter? That you think I'm made of dark magic?" she said quietly. Jin squeezed her arm, and this time she did pull away. "You weren't going to share that, Thomas? Why? Did you think it would upset me, that you think all of my people were created by *evil*?"

"You never needed to know," he said, his voice cracking a

bit, as if he was upset too. But he had no *idea* how this felt, what kind of betrayal this was to her. Even the Last Knight thought she was dangerous, after everything she'd done? "I just couldn't have you coming along, not on this mission. Shadow magic is insidious, and will exploit any weakness it can find. Your people already have a connection to it, and—"

"And so I can't be trusted," Lena said, anger and sadness now mixing in her stomach, making her want to throw up. "I get it now. You're right. Who knows what I would do if the shadow magic took me over. Maybe put a fist through a building." She pulled back and launched a punch right at the knight's house but stopped short just before it hit. "Whoa, look at that: I almost hit it since I'm so out of control!"

"Lena, I know you're upset, and you have every right to be—"

"Oh, do I? I have your permission?"

He groaned in frustration, then grabbed her by the shoulders. "Please, Lena! I *do* trust you—you know I do! But this mission is already probably doomed to fail, and I couldn't . . . If I lost you to the shadow too, along with my own people . . ."

His words set Lena back, if just a bit. *Was* he actually

worried about her? He did seem strangely upset. . . .

"Were your people made from shadow magic too, then?" Jin asked Thomas, and Lena's eyes widened in surprise at the genie's bluntness. "Stands to reason, doesn't it? Giants got big; Lilliputians got small."

"I've asked myself the same question," the knight admitted. "The fairy queens claim it was just the giants, goblins, and ogres, those kind of mons—I mean—"

Lena's eyes widened. "Those kind of what, Thomas? *Monsters?* Was that what you were going to say?"

He straightened up, then sighed deeply. "Yes, it was," he said. "I have no excuse."

"Liar!" Jin shouted. "Don't deny it. You *were* going to say monsters—*oh*. You admitted it."

"And it was incredibly wrong of me," the knight said, shaking his head. "Again, I'm so sorry. I didn't intend any of this, especially now, just before I go. Lena—"

"You know, Jin said you couldn't be trusted," she said, her insides twisting even more with every word the knight said.

"Whoa, hey!" Jin said, waving his hands at her side. "Don't say it to his *face!*"

"But *I* defended you," Lena continued, "even after he

came ranting to me about some secret conversation he heard between you and that Lilliputian I captured."

"I wouldn't say I was ranting," Jin said, sounding indignant. "Gossiping at *worst*—"

"And now it turns out he was *right*!" Lena shouted, pushing her finger into the knight's armor, which knocked him backward several feet. "Maybe not about all of his ridiculous conspiracy theories—"

"Hey, maybe stick to attacking the Last Knight here? *He's* the one you're mad at!"

"But about the *true* Thomas," Lena said, almost sneering. "I'm so sorry I brought this monster into your city, Sir Knight. Good luck with the Golden King."

And with that, she turned and strode away, not able to even look at Thomas anymore, just needing to be away from him, from Jin, from this whole city. Rufus padded along after her, his silence a mercy for her.

Behind her, she could hear Jin yelling her name, but she didn't listen, even though he might have been right about the Last Knight all along. And what was worse, his shouting was drawing residents out to peek at her from their windows, then ducking behind curtains whenever they saw her looking.

That's right—hide from the monster, she thought. *I'm just as much a giant as my parents, so if you hate them, then you hate me, too. But don't worry. I won't stick around to make you all uncomfortable any longer.*

Part of her wasn't surprised by this. She'd hoped that once the giants accepted her, she'd finally be able to stop worrying about what people thought of her. But no, even after helping save the city from the Golden King, the humans still couldn't bring themselves to trust her people.

And now the Last Knight had added another reason for humans to hate giants. But it couldn't be true, it *couldn't.* Giants hadn't been created from shadow magic . . . had they? And if Thomas was right, what did that mean? *Did* it make Lena and her people . . . evil in some way?

The humans certainly thought so, whether true or not. And that meant she just couldn't stay here, not knowing that they only allowed it because of her size, and feared everything else about her and her kind.

Maybe this was the way it had to be, giants and humans living separately, terrified of each other. Maybe she'd been the one who was wrong all along, to try to stop humans from being afraid of giants, and vice versa.

And if the Last Knight was correct, the humans might have been right to fear giants. After all, *giants fight to show their might*. What if the shadow magic meant that giants fought . . . because they were inherently bad in some way, and *liked* it? Were they just destructive by their very nature?

Lena herself loved fighting, showing off her giant strength. But did she enjoy it because part of her came from that darkness and reveled in hurting other people? She dry heaved, hating even the idea of it, but if the Last Knight was right, then everything she thought she knew could be wrong.

She wiped her arm over her face, not wanting anyone to see her eyes watering. But there were too many windows, too many people in the streets to escape their gaze. She had to get away from the crowds, get some space of her own.

Lena quickly turned onto a side street, one that led generally in the direction of the back gate, and therefore her home. But now that she was alone, the horrible emptiness inside quickly overwhelmed her, and she slid down one of the street's walls, her hands covering her face.

"Lena is okay?" Rufus asked, headbutting her face. She'd been so lost in her own thoughts that she hadn't even realized he had followed her.

"Nope," Lena said back, though she scratched him behind his ears, just so he knew she wasn't upset with him. "Lena is *definitely* not okay."

Rufus purred slightly, and she sighed, closing her eyes. "Why did Thomas have to tell me that? I could have lived my whole life never knowing how giants were made. I just wish humans and giants could get along, and none of this mattered."

Rufus's purring continued for another moment, then paused out of nowhere. He began making an odd noise, the one he made whenever hunting bugs, almost a chattering.

"No eating anyone . . . or *anything*," Lena said automatically, having had to keep Rufus from eating Humpty one too many times. She opened her eyes to make sure her cat hadn't begun hunting the poor little egg, then gasped in surprise.

Three fairies the size of Lilliputians were hovering over her, each a different color, with shining wings and serious expressions on their tiny faces.

She blinked, not sure what to say. She'd seen these three fairies around before, almost every time she'd been in the city. But they'd never gotten this close, having been content to just watch from the rooftops. "Um, hello?"

The fairies began making some sort of melodic sounds to one

another, as if they were singing. Lena almost smiled at this, as their strangeness was a nice distraction from all the horribleness of her life currently. Were they trying to communicate? Was this how they talked, with music?

Finally, the fairies seemed to reach a decision, as they all smiled at one another, then turned back to Lena. Before she could say something, they raised their voices in song, and just like that, the entire horrible Cursed City disappeared around her.

CHAPTER 6

Lena!" Jin shouted as she walked away. "Wait! This is all the knight's fault! Come back, and I'll hold him down so you can hit him or something!"

But she either didn't hear him or just chose to ignore him, disappearing around the corner.

The Last Knight sighed. "Ugh. *That* could have gone better."

He's not incorrect, the cosmic knowledge said.

"Well, yeah," Jin said, feeling his own anger rising now. "Here's an easy way not to upset the one person who idolizes you: *don't tell her she was made by evil magic.*"

The knight growled low, then grabbed Jin by his shirt. Ordinarily Jin would have been able to turn insubstantial, but the power of the ring on the knight's finger meant he couldn't evade the man, no matter how much he might want to. "You think I liked having to say that?" the knight hissed. "This is *too important*, genie. I can't take any chances. If the Golden King succeeds in covering the world with his shadow magic, it won't matter what Lena knows or doesn't. *All* of us will be under its power. I *can't* let that happen, and if Lena came along, who knows if she'd be able to resist it?"

Jin glared back at him, knowing he should try to calm the situation down, but not caring. "*I* know. Because she's Lena! She stood up to the king of giants! The shadow magic would probably take one look at her and *run*. But this isn't about that, is it? Like Lena said, I heard you talking to that Lilliputian. You want to use the shadow to take over! Maybe *you're* the one who's been infected by the evil magic—ever think of *that*?"

The knight just stared at him for a moment, then released his shirt abruptly, dropping Jin back to the ground. He caught himself just before he hit, hovering in midair, still giving Thomas his dirtiest look.

"You know *nothing* of what you speak," Thomas said, shaking his head. "I *freed* myself of the shadow after the Wicked Queen was defeated. But those years were the most horrible of my life. The shadow creeps into every corner of your heart, making you hate anyone different from you, anyone who might not share your view of the world. It made me think the Wicked Queen was *right* to rule over this world, if just so she could keep us all separated, and let me stop being afraid all of the time!"

"So what, you think that if *you* take over, then the shadow won't pull the same trick?" Jin raised both his eyebrows. "Did you ever stop to think that maybe *you'd* become just like the Golden King?"

This isn't such a great idea, you know, the cosmic knowledge said. *He can punish you however he likes with that ring.*

"Of course I've thought about that!" the knight shouted, sounding more angry than Jin had ever heard him. "But there's more to the shadow than you know, *little genie.* And I hope you never have to find out what it actually is, for your own sake."

"Now what does *that* mean?" Jin shouted back. "Stop being vague and just tell me the truth!"

But the knight straightened up, almost in shock, like he'd realized he'd said more than he'd intended. "No, you were right before," he said quietly. "The less you children have to know, the better. I should have found some other way to keep Lena here, and I won't make the same mistake twice."

"It's a little late for *that*!" Jin said.

"I told you he was hiding things," Jill said. "He blames the shadow magic, but I think he was far more like the Wicked Queen than he'd admit!"

"You think I can't hear you, Jillian?" the knight said softly. "I still have your sword, after all. You, your brother, and that princess might have taken down the Wicked Queen, but you three failed rather dramatically against the Golden King, didn't you? *I'm* the one chance we have to stop him, and bring back your niece and nephew safely, so perhaps you should just stay out of this. Your role in this story has ended."

"Ended? I'm just *starting*, Thomas," Jill growled, getting right up in his face, in spite of having no physical substance whatsoever. "Just you wait—I'm going to save the world, and if I have to do it through this sadly not very bright genie, then that's a sacrifice I'm willing to make!"

Jin rolled his eyes, not even willing to get into *that*.

"I don't have time for this," the knight said, rudely stepping right through Jill to face Jin once more. "All I would ask from you, Jin, is for your help."

"Oh, with what?" Jin asked. "Devastating Lena again? Should I tell her she's actually a goblin or something?"

"I *believe* I still have two wishes remaining, correct?" the knight hissed, his anger rising once again.

Jin started to say something snarky but stopped himself before making things worse. The cosmic knowledge wasn't wrong: the Last Knight did have the power to make Jin's life *very* uncomfortable if he wanted, just like the Golden King had. "Yes, that's right."

"First, I wish for you to evacuate the citizens of the Cursed City to my mountain cave," the knight said. "As I mentioned, they won't be safe there forever, if we can't stop the Golden King, but it could buy me a bit more time. Please make sure they're protected as best you can."

Jin blinked, surprised that the knight had gone for his suggestion with everything that had come after. Teleporting the city's residents to the mountain was *easy*, and something Jin could do with his present magic, no problem.

"I'll get it done immediately, before you even have time to wonder if you should have wished for something harder," Jin said quickly. "That means you've got one more wish, and while you don't have to rush into it, I'd say sometimes rushing actually makes your wish *more* meaningful, as it's—"

"For my third, I formally wish for you to keep Lena safe until the threat of the Golden King is finished," the knight said.

Even after all the arguing and sniping, Jin almost laughed

out loud in joy. The knight had made his *third and final wish.*
And not only did that mean Jin would be free of his control
once the wishes were completed, but the third wish meant Jin
had every excuse in the world to stay by Lena's side, from now
until . . . well, forever, if the knight failed to beat the Golden
King. And considering the knight's odds, that was looking
more likely every moment!

"I will fulfill your final wish with all the power I hold," Jin
said, bowing low before him. "And I thank you for trusting me
with your request. I—"

And then he stopped as something caught his attention.

Magic. Someone had just cast a spell of some kind. But not
like his own, or even any magic he'd seen from Mrs. Hubbard
or the other residents.

This was different, something new, something that made
the hairs on the back of his neck stand up. And that did *not*
bode well.

"See that you do," the knight said with a nod, having not
noticed apparently. "And now I need to leave, while we still
have time. The fairy queens said the king is but three days away
from covering the world with his shadow magic, and I'll need
every minute of that to coordinate with my people who are

free. Please get the evacuation started as soon as possible."

"I'm on it," Jin said, nodding absently, still distracted by the magic he'd just sensed. Who could have cast it? And for what purpose?

As the knight left to go back into his house, Jill moved over to Jin's side. "What's got you so distracted? I mean, beyond the knight being horrible, and all that stuff about giants being evil? Wait, is it the fact the world is going to end? Because that seems like it might be bad too." She shrugged.

"Something just happened, something magical," Jin said to her, glancing around to try to pinpoint it. "It was like a song of some kind. I think it's more—"

Jill cringed. "Fairy magic," she said, sending another cold wave of fear down Jin's spine. "But I'm not sensing a fairy queen. It could be the fairies that have been hanging around the city for whatever reason. Probably to watch over Sir Thomas the Sketchy, since it sounds like he's not listening to the fairy queens."

"You're *sure* it's not a queen?" Jin asked, feeling a cold chill run down his spine. "Thomas said one was just here. Do you think she'd have stuck around? Could she still be here?"

"What are you so afraid of?" Jill said. "Sure, they hate you, but it's not like they're bad people. Snotty, yes, and completely elitist, but they're on our side. Or maybe we're on their side—it's hard to know. Besides, if they were coming for *you*, you'd be gone already. Disappeared, just like that." She snapped, making him jump.

"Thanks, you're a huge help," Jin said to her.

"I wonder what the fairies are doing, if not messing with the knight?" Jill said absently. "Eh, the city's got a lot of residents. They're probably after someone we don't care about."

CHAPTER 7

Lena gaped as the Cursed City vanished from all around her, replaced by a multicolored tile path leading toward what looked like the biggest tree she'd ever seen, so large it was bigger than the Golden King's castle, and far more beautiful. Enormous crystals shone throughout the branches, almost like they'd grown there.

Um, what had just happened? Where was Rufus? And just as important, where was *she*?

And why was there a human-sized girl with golden skin and hair flying toward her on wings almost twice as big as the girl's body?

"Finally," the girl said as she landed, shaking her head. Even her clothes shimmered like gold, and for a moment, Lena

was reminded way too much of the Golden King. "You were almost late, and you have no idea how much they hate that." She looked Lena over, then frowned. "Human?"

"I'm . . . *no*," Lena said. "Giant."

The girl snorted, then stared at her more closely. "Wait, you're not joking, are you? You're *actually* a giant?"

This conversation was bringing up far too many bad feelings for Lena to let it continue. "Where am I?" she asked, pushing to her feet. "What is this place? Who are you?"

The girl sighed. "Did the fairies not tell you any of this? So irresponsible. And I should know, I used to be one of them." She grinned smugly. "Now I'm a fairy *princess*. Don't worry— you don't have to bow, or call me Your Majesty or anything. But if you do, I won't be mad."

"A fairy princess?" Lena said, even more confused now. "I thought fairies had queens."

The golden girl rolled her eyes. "We do, eleven of them. But there's been an open spot for a *long* time now, ever since one of them fell in love with the king of the merfolk. And because *I* did such great work with some of your kind—oh, I meant humans, not giants—I got promoted!" She put a hand above her head. "And, you know, enlarged, from regular fairy size. When I finally get to be a fairy queen, they should add a few more feet of height."

"I don't . . . what?" Lena said. "What does this have to do with me?"

"It doesn't." The girl sniffed. "I don't even know who you are, tiny giant girl. I'm just here to bring you to the fairy queens, not to get your life story." She waved for Lena to follow her, then turned, leapt into the air, and began flying slowly toward the huge tree in the distance.

"The fairy queens want to see me?" Lena asked, hurrying to catch up as she wondered what reason they could have for bringing her here. And then something horrible occurred to her. "Is this because . . . I'm made from shadow magic?"

The fairy princess stopped in midair and turned around with wide eyes. "Right, the giants! I hadn't really thought about that." She squinted at Lena, then raised an eyebrow. "You don't *seem* evil. Are you hiding it or something?"

"Not exactly," Lena said, her anger quickly returning. "I just found out a few minutes ago."

"Oh don't worry, I won't judge," the fairy princess said, and resumed her flight. "Who cares if you're made from evil magic, I say. That makes you a thousand times more interesting than those boring, regular humans."

"Oh, well then, if I'm more interesting, then I'm *so okay* with being made from darkness," Lena growled sarcastically, and the fairy laughed.

"*Definitely* more interesting," she said. "Anyway, most people end up here because they wished for something. So what's your wish?"

"My wish?" Lena said, not sure where that question had come from. "I don't have a . . . Oh, I guess I made one, back in the Cursed City. Wait, is *that* really why I'm here?"

The fairy glanced back over her shoulder. "Usually, but who knows? You're the first giant who's ever been here, so it could be anything. I've met a few giants myself, by the way. One tried to eat me and the dangerously inept human I was guarding. Saving him over and over is what got me promoted."

"Oh, I'm . . . sorry about that?" Lena said, almost more confused now.

"Thank you," the fairy said, stopping again to smile at Lena. "Not enough people have sympathy for everything I went through with that human!" Having apparently misinterpreted Lena's apology, the fairy princess shuddered. "You can't even imagine, trust me."

"Okay," Lena said, if just to appease the girl. "So if you don't know why the fairy queens wanted me, how did you know I'd be here?"

"Oh, it's in the Tales," the girl said. "*Everything's* in that book."

"A book?" Lena asked. "You mean like a Story Book?"

The fairy princess snorted. "Those old things? The fairy queens stopped making them a hundred years ago. I'd be surprised if any are still around now. Though I do hear that some humans are making their own, non-magical Story Books."

"So what is this Tales book, then?"

"Only the sum total of everything that has happened and will happen, little giant!" the fairy said proudly. "It's the greatest creation of the fairy queens, an account of all the things you earthbound people get up to. Have you ever gotten a prophecy about anything?"

Lena winced, remembering the ridiculous prophecy her mirror had given her back before the Golden King's invasion. "Sort of. But I didn't like it."

"Yeah, well, you people never do," the fairy said with a shrug. "Always trying to escape your destiny. Oh, I'm not judging, I would too, if I wasn't destined for such great things!" She grinned. "*The Tales of All Things* is where those prophecies come from. And that's why you're here, because the Tales said you needed to be. But you're not allowed to see the book yourself, so don't ask." She gave Lena a closer look. "Unless you ask nicely, and call me Your Majesty. In that case, maybe I'd sneak you in to see the book."

"That's okay, um, Your Majesty," Lena said, and the girl beamed.

"Wow, that really does suit me," she said. "So you didn't tell me your wish."

"It wasn't anything that impressive."

"You wanted to find your prince, right?" the fairy said. "That's what most people wish for, a prince or princess. They *say* it's true love, but really they just want to marry royalty and get rich. It's all a scam."

Lena crinkled her nose. "Ugh, no. I didn't wish for anything like that."

The fairy raised an eyebrow. "Seriously? Nothing about a prince? A princess, then?"

"No, neither," Lena said, shaking her head. "I don't care about that stuff. It's never . . . I don't know—I just wasn't ever interested in people that way."

"Oh, giant girl, you're the most fascinating creature I've met in *years*," the fairy said, her eyes lighting up. "You've *got* to tell me your wish now."

Lena looked away. "It's not going to happen, so it doesn't matter."

"Look where you are. This is the fairy homelands, and you don't just show up here to have your wish *not* granted. Tell me!"

Lena bit her lip, then nodded. "I just . . . I wished for humans and giants to not hate and fear each other, okay?"

The fairy just stared at her for a moment, then burst out laughing. "No way. Really? You'd probably have a better chance with a prince or princess, honestly!"

Anger erupted in Lena's chest, and she had to stop herself from grabbing the fairy by her golden dress and shaking her until she stopped laughing. "You *asked*. And it's *not* funny!"

The fairy stopped laughing abruptly, and she sighed. "You're right, I did ask. And it's not funny, no. It's just . . . I've met humans, and I've met giants. And neither one seems smart enough to get along with the other."

Lena couldn't deny *that*, so she just stayed silent. The fairy mercifully did the same, and they continued their journey toward the tree.

Except just as they reached it, the entire land shifted, like someone had turned a page and replaced the tree with a castle made entirely of crystal, almost too stunning to look at. Lena covered her eyes with her forearm as the sunlight shone through every facet of the castle, struggling to see where the fairy princess was now. Fortunately, the fairy grabbed her sleeve and helped guide her.

"Sorry about that," the fairy said. "It likes to show off at the worst possible moments."

"What likes to show off?"

"The castle, of course." And with that, she led Lena over a drawbridge and inside the crystalline castle.

As they went, the scene shifted again, now revealing an ocean view just outside the windows, where before there had been only trees and fields. "What *is* this place?" Lena asked, not able to hide her amazement.

"I know, it's impressive," the golden fairy said. "Most fairies have to work their whole lives to even be allowed in the homelands, so you're lucky to see it. We should hurry, though, so you're not late. That'd be *my* fault, as I shouldn't have gotten so distracted by you."

They reached a pair of enormous doors, and the golden fairy knocked quietly, almost too silent to hear. But the doors instantly pushed open, revealing an enormous room made entirely from crystal, with twelve thrones arranged in a semi-circle. Eleven of them were occupied by impossibly tall, majestic creatures that had to be the fairy queens, even though none of them had wings like the princess who'd brought her here.

"Good luck," the fairy said. "By the way, I didn't get your name."

"Lena," she whispered, then without even thinking about it, followed up with: "And what's yours?"

"Gwentell," the golden fairy said with a strange sort of smile. "Hope to see you again, Lena. Now go have your wish fulfilled, or whatever it is that brought you here!"

Lena nodded, too nervous to say anything else, then stepped into the throne room.

All eleven women stared down at her without even a hint of warmth, and Lena couldn't help but be reminded of how the king of giants had looked at her so coldly during the Spark ceremony. The fairy queens had told Thomas giants were created from evil. Was she here to be punished for that? Sent back to the clouds and never allowed to leave?

She bowed low, not sure what else to do.

"Your manners serve you well, little giant," a fairy queen in blue said from the center of the semicircle. "We apologize for the manner of your arrival, but our need is desperate, and you are the only one who can help us. You must *stop* the Last Knight, before he dooms the entire world."

CHAPTER 8

The evacuation didn't take long. In fact, Jin would have been done even faster if he hadn't had to stop and explain it over and over.

"It's to keep you safe, okay?" Jin shouted for the seventeenth time as he dropped the last resident, the Frog Prince, off at the cave's mouth. Why couldn't these humans—cursed or otherwise—just trust that he was removing them from their various homes, stores, or the Cursed City's streets to hide them in a cave for a good reason?

"You heard him," Mr. Ralph said, helping to bring people farther inside the cave. Jin had realized after the first few groups that it helped to have some allies, so he had enlisted a few friends in the Cursed City's guards. "Last Knight's orders. The Golden King has sent his shadow magic after us, and while the knight tries to stop it, we have to give him as much time as we can."

"Mama, I'm scared!" one of Mrs. Hubbard's kids said to the old woman, and Jin groaned loudly.

"The Last Knight is going to take care of it, okay?" he said, probably lying, but not having any more patience. After all, at this point he'd teleported the entire population of the Cursed City into the knight's cave, and he still hadn't managed to find the one person he cared about. "Has anyone seen Lena, though?"

"Not since earlier," Mrs. Hubbard said.

"Anyone else?" Jin shouted, getting more worried now.

The residents all looked at one another, then shook their heads. This was *not* good. What if Lena was in danger somewhere? Could she have been captured by the Faceless, or gone after the Last Knight alone? Neither seemed likely, but they were both better than the one possibility Jin didn't even want to consider.

You're so worried because of the knight's third wish, right? the cosmic knowledge asked. *Not because of any feelings you might have for her?*

Jin blinked, then nodded. *Of course because of the wish.*

Now why don't you put all that knowledge to good use and find *her for me?*

You don't need me to. You already know where she is. That's why you're so anxious.

Jin swore softly, then teleported back to the city.

Jill was waiting for him when he arrived. "You know, I'm starting to think that fairy magic might have been about *Lena*," she said. Rufus, Lena's cat, was sitting at her feet looking worried, which did not help Jin's mood in the least.

"I figured that out *so* long ago," Jin lied, not liking this at all. Fairies hated genies, and him fighting the fairy queens to rescue Lena wasn't going to improve that opinion.

You couldn't even handle one *fairy queen, let alone eleven.*

Not helping! "The more important question is," Jin said, feeling around with his magical senses, "*where* did they take her?" He turned to Rufus. "What did you see, cat?"

"Lena disappeared," the annoying cat said sadly, his whiskers drooping. "Lena leave Rufus *behind*."

Jin rolled his eyes and pulled off Rufus's magical hat that enabled the cat to speak. "I think I'd like you more if you were quiet."

Rufus narrowed his eyes. "Oh, is that so, foul one?"

he meowed at Jin, who was shocked to discover he could understand the cat's natural language. "Perhaps I should teach you a lesson with my claws of death, that you might come to respect me as I deserve?"

Jin blinked. "Um, what?"

"The glittering fairykin sent her somewhere, taking my heart and my soul with her," Rufus continued. "I swear, if I so much as see one of their kind, I shall rend them wing from wing."

Jin glanced down at the magical hat in his hand, then put it back on Rufus's head. "I was wrong," he said. "I prefer you this way."

"Genie is strange," Rufus said in the human language now, and Jin couldn't help but be a bit less impressed by how badly the hat translated his meows. Still, there were far more important things to worry about at the moment.

"If only there was some way to know where the fairies took her!" Jin said, getting back to Jill. "Maybe I could sense a magical trail of some kind? Or travel back in time to witness her kidnapping myself?"

Jill shrugged, then pointed up at a nearby roof. "We could just ask them, I suppose."

Jin glanced up in surprise, just in time to see three tiny

fairies duck behind the roof's chimney. He growled deep and low, then teleported himself and Jill up to the roof behind the chimney, leaving Rufus behind so he wouldn't eat any of the fairies before Jin could question them.

As soon as he and Jill appeared, the fairies bolted, but Jin managed to grab the nearest fairy, an orange one, before it could escape. The other two, purple and green, took to the air, leaving their friend all alone.

And that suited Jin just fine.

"*Where is she?*" he roared, changing his voice to a dragon's to be more intimidating.

The fairy snorted, then promptly bit him.

Jin screamed in surprise and pain, immediately dropping the fairy.

"I will tell you *nothing*, djinn!" the tiny orange fairy shouted in her own musical language, her hands on her hips as she glared darkly. "Touch me again, and I'll make you wish you'd never been born, or split off from another of your kind, whatever you horrible creatures do!"

Jin just stared at the little creature in disbelief. "Did you hear what she just said?" he demanded of Jill.

"Oh yeah, they're all like that," Jill said. "There was one

named Gwentell that just *hated* my brother, which honestly I kind of respect. But wow did she get on my nerves. It's not as bad for normal people, because you have to be pretty magical to be able to understand their language."

"Lady Gwentell could fly *circles* around you, *ghost*," the fairy said, shooting her death glare at Jill this time.

"Oh really?" Jill shouted back, forcing a laugh. "Let's see how tough you talk after I tie you up and throw you down a well, you little—" She leapt forward and made a grab for the fairy, only for her hands to slide right through the creature. "Oh, *come on*. I should be able to touch magical creatures!"

The fairy stuck out her tongue, then zapped Jill with a bolt of lightning, making the ghost shout in pain, then swear under her breath. "That hurt!" Jill sounded surprised. "Jin, *get her!*"

Jin nodded, trying to figure out how exactly to do that, when the cosmic knowledge decided to butt in. *Perhaps you're going about this the wrong way, maybe? We know that fairies and genies don't tend to get along, from what you've read in those Story Books. But that doesn't mean a diplomatic approach couldn't still work.*

Unless by diplomatic you mean 'chew her up and spit her out,' then no, I don't think I should try that! Jin thought back.

This anger isn't helping your case, the cosmic knowledge replied. *While they might not like* you, *they'd have had no reason to harm Lena. As Jill mentioned, the fairy queens seem to be on the side of good more often than not in all the stories. So perhaps they mean to help her?*

If you know so much, where did they take her? I'll just teleport there and rescue her!

The cosmic knowledge laughed, never a good sign. *She must be in the fairy homelands. So, go for it! Let's see how that works out for you.*

Jin didn't care for the cosmic knowledge's tone, so he chose to ignore it. "I bet you took my friend to the fairy homelands!" he shouted at the fairy. "That means I just need to teleport there and take her back. So there!" And then he stuck out his own tongue at her.

Now the fairy laughed, which didn't help Jin's confidence much. "You really are the most djinn of all djinns," she said, wiping a tear away as she continued giggling. "Your kind can't *use* fairy magic. There's no way for you to get to the homelands."

And there *we go,* the cosmic knowledge said. *Fairy magic is controlled via music, usually by singing or humming. It's completely incompatible with genie magic.*

"Oh, I can sing my magic if I *want*," Jin said, then took a deep breath.

> "Let me go to the fairy homelands,
>
> so I can get my friend home *AND!*
>
> Then bring her *back*,
>
> So I don't have to *attack*!"

The fairy's mouth dropped open in surprise.

Then she began laughing even harder, which again, didn't help Jin's mood. Meanwhile, Jill just slapped her forehead. "Really?" she said.

"What?" Jin asked, not understanding why it hadn't worked. "They use musical magic, right? So I sang my spell!"

"It takes more than some bad rhymes and singing off-key!" Jill shouted. "Their spells are the *melody*, not the words. But you're lucky that I actually know the right song to get us there."

"No you *don't*," the fairy said, rolling her eyes. "You're no chosen one, and none of the fairy queens would have ever agreed to be *your* godmother. They never would have let you in."

"Oh, I wasn't *let* in," Jill said, poking her own chest as she leaned in close to the fairy. "I *broke* in, back when I worked for the Wicked Queen!"

The fairy gasped at this, then squinted up at Jill. "Wait, that's who you are!" she shouted, her face contorting with anger. "The horrible, stinky sister of Gwentell's human!"

Jill swatted out at the fairy uselessly, then yelped as the fairy shocked her again. "I am *not stinky*!" she shouted.

Jin just shook his head at all of this. "If you know the spell to get there, Jill, maybe share it? I want to get to the homelands before anything happens to Lena!"

"You'll never get anywhere *near* the homelands!" the fairy said, slowly rising into the air, her hands held out before her like she was ready to fight.

Again, I'd suggest being more diplomatic here, the cosmic knowledge said. *She might be small, but fairykin are made of magic, just as you are. And* they *aren't held back by their full powers not coming for another thousand years.*

Oh come on, Jin thought back. *She's, like, six inches tall. I think I can take her.*

Oh, then be my guest. This should be fun.

On *that* foreboding note, Jin waved his hand for the fairy to take her shot. "Let's see it, then! Stop me. I dare you." He de-solidified his hand, then moved it through the fairy, just as Jill had done. "Can't even bite me this time, can you?"

The fairy responded by jolting him with a tiny bolt of

lightning as well, which did sting a bit, but wasn't as bad as he'd expected. Certainly nothing he couldn't handle.

Then another bolt of electricity hit him in the back. And another, and *another*.

"Um, Jill?" Jin said, his hair now standing on end as his body spasmed over and over. "Tell ME those OTHER two fairies DIDN'T come BACK to HELP her?"

Jill looked over his shoulder, and her eyes widened. "Um, not exactly."

"Good," Jin said, taking a deep breath to try to regain control of his physical form.

"It's more like they came back and brought a *bunch* of friends," Jill said quickly.

Jin winced, then slowly turned around to find easily two dozen of the tiny fairies hovering in the air, each of them buzzing with electricity as they faced him.

"You think we weren't prepared for you, djinn?" the original fairy asked, flying over to join her friends. "We were warned you might try to interfere, and have orders in that case."

Several of the fairies cracked their knuckles.

"Hey, wait!" Jin said, throwing up his hands in surrender. "Can't we be diplomatic about this? We're all made of magic here, so I bet if we really tried, we could come up with a solution that everyone could agree on—"

"Get him!" the original fairy yelled, and Jin screamed as a veritable wave of lightning bolts slammed into his body, making everything go dark.

CHAPTER 9

You want me to *stop* the Last Knight?" Lena said, her eyes widening. "But . . . why? He's trying to keep the Golden King from spreading shadow magic over the world. Why would you want me to *stop* that?"

The fairy queen in blue gave her a sympathetic look. "You do not have the benefit of foresight as we do, child. We have seen how this story plays out. To defeat the Golden King, the Last Knight will try to take control of the shadow magic himself, and it will consume him *utterly*. He believes he is strong enough to fight it, but no mortal can do so. You must act to imprison the shadow, and keep it from the Last Knight, or it will be Sir Thomas himself who covers the world in darkness."

Lena's heart began to race, and she couldn't believe what she was hearing. Jin had warned her of this same thing, and she hadn't believed him at the time. But these were the queens of the fairies, the same ones that Thomas said had warned him about the Golden King's plan to begin with.

Could they be wrong about everything, both Thomas's intentions and how giants came to be? It was possible, but Lena knew it also could just be wishful thinking on her part.

But how could the Last Knight take such a risk? Especially after claiming Lena herself was *so* vulnerable to the shadow? It didn't make any sense . . . unless there was no other way.

"Maybe he has a good reason?" Lena blurted out, not sure what else to say.

"He does believe he is out of options, yes," the blue fairy queen said. "And he hopes that he'll be able to resist the shadow's call, to use the magic for good. The knight *is* a decent person, but not even he can stand against the power of the shadow. We more than anyone know this to be true, as we have fought against the dark magic since it first appeared in our world." She gestured at the other fairy queens, who nodded. "We cannot allow Sir Thomas to unleash it once more."

"But that's what the Golden King is planning on doing himself!" Lena said, knowing she was probably being rude to these majestic creatures, but not able to help herself. "If you

72

keep the knight from stopping him, how is that going to end any better?"

"Because the Golden King *will* be defeated, but not by the knight," a fairy queen in red said. "*You* will be the hero to vanquish him, little giant."

Lena's eyes widened. *Her?* Sure, she firmly believed she could take the Golden King down, regardless of his magic, but Thomas hadn't even considered her help due to the shadow. How could the fairy queens be willing to trust her, when Thomas couldn't?

"But Thomas said the shadow could exploit something in me," she said quietly. "I'm . . . I'm a giant. The knight said that we were . . . that the shadow magic—"

"It is true that giants were created by the darkness," a fairy queen in purple said, and Lena felt like she'd just been stabbed. "And that *will* make you vulnerable. But what evil creates, goodness can redeem."

Lena almost didn't hear the words, she felt so sick. It turned out Thomas was exactly right: the fairy queens *did* think she was wrong somehow, down to her core. A mixture of disbelief and shame crashed over Lena like a tidal wave, and she had to clench her fists hard not to scream out how wrong they all were, how she *wasn't* a bad person, no matter what had created giants.

All she'd ever wanted was to be seen as a true giant. And now the world was set on taking even that from her, insisting that giants were evil somehow. And maybe some were, like King Denir. But not her parents, not Creel the Sparktender, who'd given her the epithet of Lena the Giant.

"I'll beat the shadow magic, then," she said finally, forcing her voice to sound confident, even if she didn't feel it. "I can do it. I *know* I can!"

"You can't, child," said the fairy queen in white.

What? Now they didn't think she could do it? But they'd just said—

"Only light can stand against shadow," the fairy queen in blue said, holding out her hand. She hummed for a moment, and a blue candle shimmered into existence. "This is the Illumination of Worthiness, a candle whose flame will temporarily send the shadow fleeing. As its name suggests, it will spark into flame only for someone truly noble, which we believe you have the potential to be."

"The potential?" Lena said, clenching her fists to try to keep her hands from shaking. It didn't work.

74

"You shall face three trials on your journey," the fairy queen in blue continued. "If you can successfully prove yourself during these challenges, the candle shall know your worth, and burst into flame at your touch. Skip or fail them, and you will never light the Illumination of Worthiness, without which you will have no chance against the darkness."

"What sort of trials are they?" Lena asked, her voice cracking as she spoke.

"The first shall be the Trial of Wrath," the fairy queen in purple said. "You must rise above your rage and anger, as these are tools of the shadow."

"The second shall be the Trial of Warfare," the fairy queen in red said. "You must show you love peace above all else, and resist the urge toward violence and fighting."

"And the third shall be the Trial of Wickedness," said the fairy queen in blue. "Will you choose to rise above the giant you have been, and become something better, something *worthy*? Only then will the Illumination of Worthiness light for you, enabling you to defeat the shadow and imprison it *forever*."

And with that, the fairy queen in blue handed Lena the candle. For a brief moment, Lena felt a tiny spark of hope that it would light up at her touch, but as she took the Illumination of Worthiness in her hand, it remained dark and unlit, proving what the fairy queens had said was true.

She . . . wasn't worthy. Because she was a giant, and therefore created by evil, something inside her wasn't right, wasn't *good*. Maybe that explained why she liked to fight so much, why the Cursed City residents didn't trust her kind.

But hadn't it been her strength, her *might*, that had helped save her friends during the Golden King's last attack? Didn't that mean it was useful, worthy in some way?

Or was that the fairy queens' point, that goodness could redeem evil? That explained the trials, as her actions would count for far more than just having good intentions.

She opened her mouth to respond, but the fairy queen in blue raised a hand to stop her. "I know this is hard for you, young Lena. We never want to believe the worst about ourselves and our loved ones. But the future has been written, and it is quite clear: to defeat the Golden King, you must journey through the shadowlands and pass the three trials within. The shadow will try to tempt you, to terrify you with your greatest fear, looking for whatever weakness it can exploit. You can beat it, child, but only with the help of the Illumination of Worthiness. And for that, you must rise up, prove that you can be *more* than a giant, not held down by your base instincts, the *destructiveness* inherent to your kind."

Your base instincts . . . destructiveness *inherent to your kind.* The fairy queen's words hit Lena like a blow to the stomach, and she wanted to run, to hide, anything to not have to listen to any more of this.

But the fairy queens said that the world depended on her, depended on Lena proving her worth. And she couldn't let it be taken over by the shadow, the darkness, not when she could stop it.

But maybe there was another way? Some path they hadn't thought of?

"Perhaps it is time to show you how we know these things," the fairy queen in blue said, apparently reading her mind. She beckoned Lena forward as she began humming softly. This time, an enormous book that looked thousands of years old appeared in the air between them and opened its pages. Lena gasped, figuring this was the book the fairy princess Gwentell had mentioned.

She slowly peered over the upside-down pages, not sure what to expect, but whatever language the book had been written in was nothing Lena had ever seen before.

The fairy queen, however, seemed to have no problem with it.

"'As it has been written in *The Tales of All Things*,'" she read, "'the Giant Who Is Not shall imprison the Chaos once and for all by journeying through the lands of Shadow, led by the Boy Who Was Freed and protected by the Ever-Changing One. She will light the darkness with the Illumination of Worthiness, won for her by passing three trials: a Trial of Wrath, a Trial of Warfare, and a Trial of Wickedness. Failing these will leave her defenseless, and spell certain doom for the world.

"'However, if she be found worthy, she will defeat the darkness, and the Giant Who Is Not shall retrieve the Prison of Light from the King Made of Gold, who has hidden it away, and imprison the Shadow within.

"'If the darkness be successfully contained within the Prison of Light, the world shall forevermore be free of its horrible power. If, however, the Knight of the Thumb steals the Shadow and wields it instead, *The Tales of All Things* shall be rewritten, and all shall be lost.'"

And with that, the blue fairy looked up at Lena expectantly. So did the ten other fairy queens.

Lena couldn't breathe, couldn't even speak for a moment, and just had to turn her gaze down to the book while the fairy queens waited. Three trials, one each for the anger, violence, and evil inside her. And if she failed them, the world would be doomed.

"Where does this book come from?" she asked, trying not to think about the pressure and shame she was feeling. "How does it know the future?"

The fairy queens began to laugh quietly, making Lena's face heat up. "*The Tales of All Things* was created from the sum total of all fairy magic," the blue fairy queen said. "These pages simply contain the story of what must come to pass if the future is to be one of goodness and light. Our sacred responsibility is to ensure that the Tales happen just as they're meant to, or we will have failed the world and let darkness overcome us all." She smiled gently.

"But you are all so powerful, couldn't you stop the shadow if I . . . fail?" Lena asked, almost choking on the last word

"Our power is great, but nothing next to the shadow," the fairy queen in purple said, and the others all nodded silently. "It disrupts the Tales, changes things, sends them off in new, dangerous directions. The last time we directly faced the darkness, we inadvertently caused this present danger."

"The shadow is pure chaos," the fairy queen in blue said. "The more we interfere, the worse its disruption becomes. If we attempted to face the Golden King directly, the outcome could be catastrophic."

"No, the Tales are quite clear on this matter," a fairy queen in white said. "*You* are the chosen one, and you alone are able to stop the Golden King, and by doing so, keep the Last Knight from a truly world-ending error. Now, what will you do? Abandon the world to its fate, or prove yourself worthy and save us all?"

Lena swallowed hard. It made her sick to think that the fairy queens' claims about giants were true, but between the candle not lighting and the sheer powerful presence of the women, she couldn't help but believe their words.

If she was the only one who could save the world, and to do so meant denying her giant heritage, then . . . then . . .

"I'll do it," she said quietly, barely able to get the words out. "However I need to, whatever trials I need to pass, I will. I won't let the shadow hurt anyone else."

The fairy queens all smiled, and a few let out a sigh of

relief. "Thank you, child," the fairy queen in blue said. "We understand how hard it will be to rise above your own impulses, but you have our thanks." She held up a hand, and a page of writing appeared within it. "Take this. It's the prophecy I just read to you from *The Tales of All Things*. Let it guide you, and help save us all."

Her thoughts racing in a thousand different directions, Lena nodded and took the page. Not able to look at it, she folded it and put it in her infinitely large pouch for safekeeping.

And then something occurred to her. "Wait," she said. "If I'm supposed to face these trials in the shadowlands before the candle finds me worthy, then how will I even get to them? Won't the shadow take over my mind?"

"The Boy Who Was Freed will have a way to protect you and your companions," the fairy queen in blue said. "But neither he nor the Ever-Changing One will be able to face the shadow directly and imprison it. That is your job alone." She spread her arms and hummed a note. Gwentell reappeared in the back of the room, a huge smile on her face. "But now you must go, as time is short. I apologize for not sending you back myself, but I have less . . . pleasant business to attend to at the moment. Princess Gwentell will help you on your way. Just know that you have the hope of all fairykin with you throughout your journey, young Lena."

And with that, Lena found herself outside the throne room, its doors slamming shut, alone but for Gwentell.

"So?" the fairy princess asked, her smile widening. "How did it go? I bet your wish got granted, didn't it?"

CHAPTER 10

Jin woke up to a light so bright he immediately tried to cover his eyes, only to find he couldn't move. "Hey!" he shouted, struggling against whatever was holding him down. "What *is* this?"

"Hello, little djinn," said a fairly terrifying voice, and a tall, impossibly beautiful woman stepped into view, blocking the light slightly. "My name is Merriweather. Do you know who I am?"

Uh-oh. "I, um, might have heard of you, sure," Jin said, his heart racing in fear. "You're a fairy queen who is fair and just and would never hurt a vulnerable little djinn." Jin paused. "Since that's true, I should probably let you know that some of your subjects blatantly attacked me for no reason whatsoever. I was completely minding my business, and then, bam, zap, kapow! You should really punish them, honestly."

"That isn't what happened in the slightest," Merriweather said, the light illuminating her blue dress from behind. "They had orders to not interfere with you, knowing you are part of the Tales . . . as much as your kind *can* be. So for you to be here, they must have thought you were a threat, and dealt with you accordingly."

Part of the "tails"? Did the fairies *have* tails, or worse, were they going to give *him* one?

Struggling to stay calm, he took a deep breath, trying to remember that diplomacy might still work. After all, he needed to find out what had happened to Lena, and this genie-hating fairy queen was the only one with answers.

"We'll probably never know the full truth of it," Jin said, compromising. "I suppose there's plenty of fault to go around, even if they were mostly to blame, since they took my friend first. Speaking of this new subject, where's Lena? Is she okay?"

The fairy queen smiled slightly, sending Jin's heart racing again, both from her beauty and because he suspected her smile was *not* a great sign for him. "Of course, she's quite well. We brought her here to ask for her *help*, djinn. She was never in any danger. In fact, she's most likely already on her way home."

In spite of his personal danger, Jin felt a huge sense of relief. It was one thing for the fairy queens to attack him; he couldn't die, at least not in the normal sort of way. But Lena was mortal, and therefore much more fragile.

Fragile? The girl who could throw you a mile? the cosmic knowledge said. *And fairy queens wouldn't be using "normal" ways to hurt you.*

Oh, thank you *for that! I really needed some optimism right now.* Out loud, Jin said, "Well, *that's* good news. I guess you can just send me back too, since all of our business here is done. It was great meeting you, but I really should be going, so—"

"Oh, not just yet, if it's all the same to you," the fairy queen said, and moved out of the light, blinding Jin. He groaned in pain and tried making himself insubstantial, hoping to pass through whatever bonds were holding him down, but it didn't help: somehow, he still couldn't move his body.

"It isn't all the same to me, actually," he said, turning his head to try to avoid the light, but failing completely. "Listen, I get that fairy queens don't like genies, and vice versa. But there's no reason to make this personal! I've got nothing against you, and you've never even *met* me—"

This made the fairy queen laugh, sending a horrible chill down

Jin's spine. He forced a laugh too, just so she'd know the feeling.

"Oh, we've met," Merriweather said, still staying out of the light. "Or would you consider that a former version of yourself? I'm unclear on djinn culture."

A former version? What was she talking about?

Hmm, the cosmic knowledge said. *While this probably isn't the time to explain how genies are made—*

What?! It's never *the time for that!*

But it sounds like it may be relevant. Since djinn are made of magic, your kind tend to just . . . split off from their parent, and become something altogether new. And in your situation, well, I didn't want to be the one to tell you this, but . . .

But what? Jin shouted in his head. *But what?!*

"Does this version of you remember being trapped in the mirror?" Merriweather asked, from somewhere behind him now. "Or does your memory begin from the moment you split?"

Jin's eyes slowly widened with understanding. *No way,* he said to the cosmic knowledge. *You're saying I . . . came from* that *genie? The ifrit who fought Merriweather?*

The battle took place twelve years ago, the same number of years as your age. I'd imagine that during the fight with the fairy queen, some of the ifrit's magic broke off, maybe after one of her attacks. Typically a djinn would just pull themselves back together after a battle, but given that Merriweather trapped it back in this magic mirror she mentioned, perhaps there was no time?

No time? You're saying all of this is happening, from me doing a thousand years of service—

Longer, actually.

And learning how not to be selfish, Jin continued, *to almost getting killed by various ring holders—*

You were never almost killed. Stop exaggerating. You were only put through massive amounts of pain.

All because this fairy queen cut off a piece of ifrit me? Jin finished, barely able to believe all of this.

It seems as if that's so, the knowledge told him. *However, I'd think that would be less of a concern than the fact that the same fairy queen now holds you in her power. And if I remember correctly from your reading of that Story Book, your ifrit parent almost destroyed her.*

Jin's eyes widened. *That's right, it did. So, um, it looks like I might be in trouble, then.*

It does indeed.

"First of all, the *nice* thing to do would be to forgive and forget," Jin pointed out. "And second of all, how do you know I came from that ifrit?"

Merriweather sighed. "Do you really believe me so easily fooled? I could never forget the feel of your magic."

"No, but you can't blame anything the ifrit did on me!" Jin said, struggling to turn around and face her, but having no more luck now than earlier. "Would you blame a newborn baby for what its parents did to you?"

"Not unless I knew what that baby was going to grow up to be," Merriweather said, her voice going cold. "You might not remember it, djinn, but you and I *have* met. And I'm not speaking of your ifrit sire. Perhaps you truly don't remember, but I do, as do my sisters."

What is she talking about? Jin asked the cosmic knowledge as he struggled against whatever bonds were holding him. *I've never met a fairy queen!*

For a moment, the cosmic knowledge was silent, and Jin wondered if the voice in his head had disappeared. But when it finally spoke, it almost confused him even more. *I am forbidden from revealing certain . . . truths to you. This is one of them.*

What? Is this just because I annoy you?

It isn't, though that doesn't help.

"I thought you would at least show me the proper respect, given your vulnerability here," Merriweather continued. "You are a guest in *my* home now, ifrit. There are ten other fairy queens here, ready to put you through the most intense pain you've ever felt, if you make so much as the slightest move to harm me."

"I would never try to harm any of you!" Jin shouted. "How could I, when I can't even move? And I'm *not* an ifrit! If you can sense my magic, then you should know that. I'm not even much of a regular genie. I'm like the weakest djinn *ever*."

You're not wrong.

Do you remember the last time you were helpful? Because I can't.

Merriweather blocked the light once more, staring closely at Jin. While he was thankful for not being blinded, having the fairy queen so close made him feel *way* too vulnerable. As it was, if she decided to attack him, he'd have no way to defend himself.

"Good," she said finally. "You are appropriately pathetic in your magical abilities. I see things are progressing as the Tales predicted."

"Yes, *completely* pathetic!" Jin agreed. "Not a threat at all!"

"And yet, that would change if you ever proved yourself humbled and selfless," Merriweather said, standing back up. "How do you fare on that challenge? Clearly you have not yet succeeded, but one would hope there has been *some* progress."

"Oh, there's been *so* much progress!" Jin said, not liking how she knew about the selflessness loophole in his curse to fulfill wishes for one thousand and fifty years. "I'm basically just about there, honestly. And I won't even go into how it's functionally impossible to actually be selfless when there's a reward for it, because that doesn't seem like the best argument to get into right now!"

The fairy queen tapped her chin. "I can see we'll get no honest answers out of you. Perhaps there's another way to determine the truth."

The truth? That he was trapped in an unfair curse to serve a bunch of horrible people and couldn't be free for another thousand years? That truth? "I'm shocked that you think I'd ever be less than honest! You wound me to my very core—"

"Not yet, but the day is young," the fairy queen said, smiling in what was far too happy a manner for Jin's taste. "But before we get to a possible wounding, I do have an idea. Magic should do the trick." She tilted her head, looking like she was enjoying this. "Now, this spell causes no pain in fairies, but it has never been tested on djinn, so I cannot make the same assurances for your kind. Let's find out together, shall we?"

And then she began humming.

CHAPTER 11

I bet your wish got granted, didn't it?" Gwentell had said. Lena almost laughed at how much that *hadn't* happened but held back, worried that if she started laughing about it all, she might not be able to stop. Instead, she just shook her head, not really wanting to talk about any of it yet.

The fairy's excitement seemed to fade a bit, only to return. "Oh, really? That's too bad. But don't worry—we'll figure it out."

"We?" Lena said.

"If they won't make your wish come true, then I will," Gwentell said with a shrug. "I mean, *technically* fairy princesses don't have that power, but it's not like we're forbidden from trying, so I say that pretty much gives me permission."

Lena smiled at her, a real, actual smile. She reached out and hugged the fairy, who let out a yelp of surprise, then slowly hugged back. As Lena released her, Gwentell was smiling as well. "What was *that* for?"

"It's been a horrible day," Lena said. "And it's just nice to have someone on my side, I guess."

Gwentell paused, then looked all around them. "Oh, you haven't seen anything yet," she said, giving Lena a sly glance. "Come on."

The fairy grabbed Lena's hand, then quietly sang a quick song in a language Lena couldn't understand, and the castle chamber melted away around them, replaced by a library larger than Lena would have thought possible. Shelves extended as far as the eye could see, each one easily ten times the height of a giant, and absolutely *packed* with books.

"I told you about the fairy queens' *Tales of All Things*, right?" Gwentell asked, looking a bit bored now. "Well, that's the overall story of how things should go, but it's built from the texts we keep here. These are the individual stories of every single person in your world, made by fairy queen magic. See?" She pointed at a nearby shelf, and Lena moved closer to look.

The Pied Piper of Hamelin. The Billy Goats Gruff. Peter Peter Pumpkin Eater.

This third book caught her attention, and she pulled it out, only to almost drop it in surprise when she saw the cover.

"That's my friend Peter!" she said, pointing at the picture of Peter from the Cursed City on the cover. "Is this his *actual* story?"

"Of course!" the fairy said. "Everyone's story is in here, no matter how small and boring. And the most important people, the ones who change the world in big ways, their stories are what make it into *The Tales of All Things,* mixing together to create the larger story of your world."

She flapped her large wings and took to the air, then whistled sharply. A number of regular-sized fairies came flying over, and she whispered something to them. They immediately all went off in different directions, and Gwentell gently set herself back on the floor.

"What did you ask them for?" Lena asked.

"It's impossible to find anything in here on our own. Those are the queens' librarians, and basically the only ones who know where specific books are kept. I asked them for a copy of *your* story."

"My *what*?" Lena's eyes widened. "You've got a book here about my *future*, too?"

"Not just that, but all the exciting bits from your past, as well!" Gwentell said, then quickly lowered her voice. "Don't tell the queens I did this, though. We're not allowed to show mortals their own stories. But I'm not breaking any rules if *I* read through it, and just tell you what you need to know to make everything work out okay!" She twisted her mouth back and forth. "At least I *hope* that's not breaking rules."

Lena's mouth dropped open. Her entire future was written out in a book? Yes, *The Tales of All Things* had just told her what was coming, but that had been pretty vague and all prophecy-sounding. If this new book was more detailed, more specific about what she'd have to do to beat the trials and be found worthy, that could be exactly the help she needed!

As Lena's whole body shook with anticipation and worry, one of the librarian fairies flew up, holding a book, with another carrying a second book just behind her. Lena spotted a picture of herself on the first one, with the words *Once Upon Another Time* on it. Was *that* her story?

"Whoa, looks like you've got a series!" Gwentell said, taking the *Once Upon Another Time* book from the smaller fairy and flipping through it, her eyes glowing. "The bigger stories always get fun titles, too," she said as she scanned the pages almost too fast for Lena to see, only to close the book just as quickly as she'd opened it. "Nope, not that one."

"What was that book about?" Lena asked, amazed by all of this.

"Oh, that was your story starting with the Spark ceremony and finishing after the Golden King's attack on the Cursed City," Gwentell said, then gave her a knowing smile. "You're even *more* interesting than I thought, little giant!"

Lena blushed, not sure what to say to that. "What, uh, kind of stuff was in there? Just a description of what happened? Or did it . . . you know, get into what I was, I don't know, *thinking*—"

"Thinking, feeling, *all of it*," Gwentell said, her smile widening. "But don't worry, I won't tell anyone."

Before Lena could respond, the fairy princess grabbed the remaining book, this one with Lena, Jin, and Rufus on the cover, and small humans running from them in terror. It was called *Tall Tales*, and Gwentell quickly scanned it as well, her eyes glowing.

And then she slammed it shut, her face contorted with anger.

"*What* did you just give me?" she shouted at the fairies. "That can't be the right story. It must be an earlier draft, and there's a more up-to-date version. Tell me you got the wrong book!"

The hovering fairies looked at one another, then sang something at Gwentell. She responded in an angry hum, and the fairies sang again. Finally, Gwentell sighed and waved them on, as Lena waited, not liking any of this. The librarian fairies gave Lena a long look before all flying off in separate directions. Gwentell, meanwhile, took a deep breath, let it out again, and turned back to Lena, smiling with her lips pushed tightly together.

"So, um, good news!" she said, smiling with all her teeth, like she was forcing herself to do it. "Your wish *does* get fulfilled. So that's something! And lets me off the hook, which is probably good, because I wasn't actually that sure I could do it—"

"My wish for giants and humans to get along, and stop fearing each other?" Lena asked, honestly a little shocked. "*Really?* That's amazing!"

Gwentell nodded, her eyes wider than normal. "It is, I know! But you don't have much time, so I should get you back home. Let you run off and save the world, all that fun stuff!" She pumped a fist in the air. "Yay for the world!"

"So wait," Lena said, barely able to believe it. "I save the world, too? I . . . pass the trials, beat the shadow?" She reached out and grabbed Gwentell's arms, squeezing them as gently as she could so as not to hurt the fairy princess. "Please, just tell me it all works out okay?"

Gwentell's smile faded. "I was *wrong* to show you these books. Do whatever you think is best, and let's hope it all ends . . . the way you deserve."

Lena just stared at her, not liking any of this. "What did you see in that book?" she asked, almost in a whisper.

Gwentell bit her lip. "Something I never thought was possible. Something *I* need to figure out how to deal with. And that's why I don't think I should share anything else. I have no idea what kind of consequences there will be." She winced. "Or what parts of the Tales I've already changed, even my own story . . ."

"There's nothing you can tell me?" Lena said, feeling more desperate as the fairy princess got more vague. "What about . . . could you just say if the fairy queens are right about me, about giants? Are we actually . . ." She stopped, having to swallow hard to avoid throwing up. "Did the shadow make us *evil?*"

Gwentell looked her right in the eye. "You are who you've always been, Lena, good or bad. And only *you* can say what you truly are." She looked like she wanted to say more but shut her mouth instead.

Lena dropped the fairy's arms. "I guess . . . I'll just have to hope I can pass these tests." She held up the Illumination of Worthiness candle for Gwentell to see.

The fairy's face contorted like she was in pain, but she only nodded in response.

"So what do I do now?" Lena asked, feeling lost in all of this. "I don't know the way to Lilliput, or wherever the Golden King is hiding. . . ."

"It's all in that passage from *The Tales of All Things*," Gwentell said, tapping Lena's pouch. Lena briefly wondered how the fairy knew she had the page, then realized she must have just read about it. She pulled the paper Merriweather had given her out of her pouch, and the fairy princess quickly grabbed it, scanning over the words. "This book is always so incomprehensible. I think they like it that way, so it seems more important. Okay, let me translate some of this. Jin's obviously the Ever-Changing One, which is just a fancy way of saying his genie form can be whatever he wants it to be. And you'll find this Boy Who Was Freed in the Last Knight's house. Start there." She handed the paper back, still not looking happy about something.

"Jin, the Last Knight's house, got it," Lena said, wishing Gwentell would just share whatever she was so upset about. The fairy princess did seem to want to help, but there was something she wasn't saying, and that made Lena worry even more. "I . . . I really appreciate your help. I can't begin to pay you back for all of this. But I'll do my best, whenever I can find a way—"

"No need," Gwentell said, more quietly this time. She glanced around, as if checking again to see if anyone could hear them, then reached down to hold Lena's hands in her own. "Be careful, okay?" she whispered. "Not every tale ends well for the hero."

"I'll try," Lena said, the warning making her even more nervous. "I'm a giant, remember? Pretty hard to hurt." She tapped her chest.

"You *are* a giant, Lena," Gwentell said sadly. "Never forget it."

Her words struck Lena like a punch to the gut, and she had to shut her eyes to control herself. *You're made from evil magic, Lena,* she heard the fairy princess say. *Never forget that.*

"I . . . I won't forget," she said, digging her fingernails into her palms to keep from losing it in front of the fairy princess. "I, um, I think I'm ready to go now."

Again, Gwentell seemed like she wanted to say something else, but she just shook her head and quickly started humming a song. Lena turned away as she faded out, leaving the fairy alone in the library.

"I understand now," Gwentell whispered to no one. "I get

why they don't want us reading the Tales. It makes it all *hurt* so much more." She shook her head. "This isn't right. Lena doesn't deserve this. And neither does Jin." She shuddered at the memory of his fate at the end of *Tall Tales*. "That poor, *poor* genie. Not even a final goodbye to Lena? Whoever wrote this Tale is just cruel!"

CHAPTER 12

erriweather's magic fell over Jin like a cloud of mist, and suddenly his thoughts dissolved into a weird sort of fog, along with all his stress and worries about Lena. It wasn't entirely unpleasant, but it did make thinking clearly a bit . . . more difficult. Difficulter? More difficulter? Less non-difficult?

What was going on? And also, what was going on?

"Oh, hello!" he said to the fairy queen, who was leaning over him, probably to see how her spell had gone. "I liked your spell. It made my mind go all floofy!" He giggled. "I thought you were going to torture me or something, since you hate my whole existence. But this is so much better than torture! Like twice as better!"

Merriweather didn't seem to be sharing his joy, which made

Jin sad for her. "It was only a simple spell to release your inhibitions," the fairy queen said. "It's meant to keep you from having the wherewithal to lie. But it doesn't usually have such a drastic effect."

"You know what's funny?" Jin told her. "The word 'effect.' So many people get it mixed up with 'affect,' which makes sense, because they're basically like brother and sister. Or sister and cousin? So similar!" He giggled. "But one is the result of influencing something, and the other is the act of influencing it! Pretty clever, huh?"

"What is this gibberish?" asked a new voice from farther away. Merriweather looked up, and a less-bright light replaced the blinding one, helping Jin see her better. Oddly, Merriweather looked pretty unsettled. Even more oddly, there were ten *more* fairy queens floating behind Merriweather, all watching him intently.

Jin tried to wave to them in a friendly way, not wanting them to feel left out, only to realize he still couldn't move. "Hullo!" he said instead.

"Perhaps I overdid the spell's power," Merriweather said. "I had thought the djinn's natural defenses would be . . . stronger."

"You know who's strong?" Jin asked. "*Lena*. Strong, and so cute! But also fierce, and intimidating. Grr!" He growled. "You know what's funny? The word 'grr' is an onomatopoeia, which is *also* funny." He started repeating it in a sort of singsong voice. "Onomatopoeia! Onomatopoeia? Onomatopoeia, onomato—"

"Enough!" Merriweather shouted, and magical power crackled off her. Jin gasped, then gasped again, enjoying how it sounded. Not that "gasp" was an onomatopoeia, which didn't seem fair to the word, but still. "Tell me the *truth*, genie: Have you been progressing in your challenge to be humbled? Do you bear any ill will toward the human world or its people?"

"Let me check," Jin said, feeling like he knew the answer already, but not wanting to be wrong about it. *Cosmic knowledge? How am I doing on . . . what she said?*

Weirdly, the cosmic knowledge didn't answer, which was definitely weirdly weird. And also strange. *Hello?* Jin thought again, then, for good measure, said the same thing aloud. "Hello?"

Merriweather growled. "Yes, *hello*. I'm still here, waiting for my answer."

"Oh, sorry, I was just trying to talk to the sum total of all knowledge in my head," Jin told her. "But it seems to be gone for now. You know, I wonder if it's because—"

"For some reason, you not having any knowledge in your head comes as no surprise," Merriweather said, sounding annoyed. "You still have not answered my question, djinn!"

"Right, your question!" he said, getting excited about the opportunity to say more answers. "Question. Your question." He frowned. "What was it again?"

"Do you bear any ill will—"

"That's it!" Jin interrupted. "I remember now! Nope, I have no bears, sick or well. Sorry about that. If you really need a bear, maybe I could find one for you?" He looked around conspiratorially, then whispered, "You might not know this, but I'm a *genie* and can grant wishes. Shh, don't tell anyone!"

She gritted her teeth and pushed in closer, staring him in the eye with an intensity that Jin tried to match, glaring right back at her. *"Do you intend to hurt the human world, djinn?* Yes or no?"

"No!" Jin shouted excitedly, enjoying how dramatic this was all getting. "I don't like them much, even a little bit, but why would I hurt them? Unless they were mean to me, that is. Like the Golden King. Him, I'd totally hurt—"

"He must be telling the truth," Merriweather said, turning back to the other fairy queens. "I cannot believe he'd be able to lie, not in his current state. And even a djinn has too much dignity to fake . . . *this.*"

"Ah, there's where you're *wrong*," Jin said, and Merriweather turned back in surprise. "You see, I've got *no* dignity." Her eyes narrowed in anger, but she didn't interrupt, so he quickly continued. "But also, I'm not faking right now. Although . . ." He trailed off, lost in thought.

"Although?" Merriweather said, pulling Jin's mind back to the fascinating conversation they were having.

"Yes! Although I do fake a *lot* of things!" Jin said happily. "So maybe I'm faking without knowing it? That *seems* unlikely, but would I know that I didn't know? Probably not." He tried to shrug but still couldn't move. "Like I'm faking this whole body right now. Did you know I might look like a human boy, but genies don't have a gender? I can be anything I want, and switch back and forth when I'm bored." He shifted to a feminine form, a girl with short brown hair. "See? *Hello!*"

The fairy queen sighed deeply. "It would seem that things are progressing as intended, and this interrogation was not strictly necessary. So I would offer you my . . . *apologies.*" She seemed to almost choke on the last word.

"I can have your apologies?" Jin asked, shifting back to his boy form. "Yay! I'm going to keep them in a special place forever, and look at them whenever I'm feeling down."

"I have no more time for this," Merriweather growled. "I

offer a warning, by way of apology: your friend Lena is our only chance of saving the human world from darkness, and will need your aid. You must keep her safe and help her locate the Prison of Light. But know that if you open the prison yourself, you will unleash the vast force of the shadow's power upon the world and doom us all."

Jin narrowed his eyes, wanting to sound all serious like she did. "That sounds serious, but exciting! Doom us all. Doom doom doom." He grinned, not able to stay serious. "That's a fun word, 'doom.' Did you know—"

"Enough of this, Merriweather," one of the other fairy queens said. "You clearly used too much magic."

"I assumed he was somehow hiding his true power!" Merriweather said, turning to look at the others. "I would have needed far more magic to break through the ifrit's defenses, I promise you that!"

"And yet, this one is not as powerful as his sire," said another. "Are you certain he can perform his task?"

"Will he keep the giant girl safe?" asked another.

"*The Tales of All Things* is very clear," Merriweather said. She pointed down at Jin. "This is the djinn that will travel with Lena and do what needs to be done. It will all happen just as written."

"Is someone writing something?" Jin asked. "Can I be in it? Maybe the hero who falls in love with a giant, and she totally loves him back, and—"

"Yes, he is indeed the foretold djinn," said one of the other fairy queens. "We must not interfere with him any further, or we might risk changing the story."

"I am *not* interfering," Merriweather said, sounding annoyed at the fairy queens now. *That* was fun, not having her angry at him for once! "There's no permanent harm done, and this . . . confusion will pass in a matter of hours."

"Then send him along his way," said another fairy queen. "To think, a djinn being allowed in the homelands!"

"He has seen nothing of the homelands beyond this room," Merriweather said. "And we shall continue this discussion when he has gone!"

"Gone where?" Jin asked, but Merriweather was already humming. Before Jin knew it, the fairy queens had disappeared around him, replaced by the rooftop where Jin had threatened the smaller fairies.

"Jin!" shouted a familiar voice, and, finding that he could move again, Jin picked himself up to find Jill staring at him in surprise. "They let you go?"

"Jill!" he shouted, and threw his arms out to give her a hug, only to stumble right through her and almost fall off the roof. He frowned, then whirled around. "Jill!" he shouted again, and threw his arms out to hug her, only to trip and fall on the roof.

"Um, okay," Jill said as he pushed back to his feet. "Clearly they removed your brain before sending you back."

He frowned, then pushed a finger through his head and out to the other side. "I guess they did! *Weird!*"

Jill sighed deeply. "This is going to be one of *those* kinds of days, isn't it? Did you at least find Lena?"

His eyes widened. No, he hadn't! Lena was back in the fairy homelands, most likely, so there was nothing for it, he'd just have to figure out how to get back there and rescue her. He opened his mouth to tell Jill just that, when a voice shouted up from below.

"Jin? Is that you?"

"Lena?" Jin said, then glanced down over the roof to find the giant girl waiting below, next to her enormous cat. "You're here!" He glanced back at Jill. "Look at me—I *did* find her!" He shook his head in amazement. "Sometimes I'm so great, I even surprise myself."

CHAPTER 13

Lena waited impatiently while Jin floated down to her. She was glad she'd heard his voice, or she might never have found him. What had he been doing on the roof, anyway?

"Lena is back," Rufus repeated for what must have been the tenth time, purring loudly as he continually headbutted her. He hadn't given her more than a few inches of space since she'd reappeared in town, which was fair: after disappearing on him like that, she must have worried her poor boy.

Fortunately, she'd reappeared in the same spot the fairies had taken her from, and Rufus came bounding at her the moment she called his name. She hoped he'd at least been off with Mrs. Hubbard, getting treats. Though now that she thought about it, there was no one around in the city. Were the residents just hiding from her again?

I get it, she thought at them. *You don't trust giants. I finally understand why. You think we're all made of evil. But maybe I can prove to you that we're not. Just . . . just let me try, okay? Let me try to beat these challenges and show you giants can be trusted.*

"Hullo!" Jin said, grinning widely as he reached the ground finally. "I found you! You're *back!*"

Lena tilted her head, not sure what he was talking about. "Um, I found *you.* And how did you know I was gone?"

"Because I'm on my third wish!" he said brightly. "I'm third-wishing all *over* the place."

Okay, *that* made no sense. But she didn't have time for this. They needed to stop the Golden King and only had a few days to do it. "Um, fair enough. I need your help, but first, I have to admit something."

Jin's eyes widened into dinner plates. "Admit . . . something? Like, a feeling you're having?" He looked down, toeing the dirt between them.

What was going *on* with him? "Not really. You know how I said you were right about the Last Knight before? I was just . . . *upset* at the time." And still was. "But it turns out you really are right. He's going to try to use the shadow magic himself, and it'll apparently make him do all the things the Golden King means to, only worse."

Jin's face initially fell, only to light up as she continued. "Yay! I'm so glad we agree on this finally! You're the *best*, Lena. And the Last Knight isn't. You know, the best." He stopped as if considering this. "In fact, he might be the worst, because he sort of called you a monster, and you're *not*—"

"Don't," Lena said, cringing at the reminder of Thomas's words. Somehow, they hurt just as much with Jin saying them as they had when she'd first heard them.

"'Don't' is a funny word," he told her. "Where does the second *o* go? Does it just disappear?"

She just stared at him. "What is *wrong* with you? Are you okay?"

"The *most* okay!" Jin said brightly. "Why? Oh wait, I'm being talked to." He glanced over her shoulder, then nodded. "Jill says to tell you that the fairy queens captured me and probably cast some sort of magical spell on me." He leaned in closer, conspiratorially. *"Jill's right,"* he whispered.

What? The fairy queens had taken Jin, too? "Are you all right?" she asked, grabbing him by his shoulders anxiously. "Did they do anything to you? I know fairy queens don't like genies. . . ."

He shrugged. "Oh, I'm pretty sure they liked me! We asked each other *lots* of questions, and talked about mirrors and ifrits and funny words. The only thing is now I can't hear my knowledge, so that's odd. Odd odd odd." He paused again, then laughed. "Ha, Jill is funny! Mean, but funny."

"I'm sure she is," Lena said, giving him a worried look. The fairy queens had taken his knowledge? *That* raised even more questions. At least Jin still remembered her, and apparently the Invisible Cloud of Hate that he kept calling Jill, too, so that was something. "We'll figure out what the fairy queens wanted with you later, okay? Hopefully when your knowledge comes back. In the meantime, I need you to *focus*."

He squinted at her. "Done. I can even extra focus if I just change to eagle eyes—"

"That's okay!" Lena shouted, already too late as his eyes turned a golden yellow. "I meant concentrate. Can you do that?"

He scrunched up his forehead and closed his eyes. "Of course! I'm concentrating *so hard* right now." He began to whisper "concentrate, concentrate" over and over, and Lena sighed loudly.

"Just come with me," she said, and grabbed his hand. He

squealed in delight for some reason but floated along just behind her as she pulled him toward Thomas's house.

"You know, I was going to tell you something about your big cat in boots," he said from behind her. "Something big. Monumental. *Giant*, even!"

About Rufus? "What was it?"

"He can talk!"

"I can talk," Rufus confirmed. "Lena knows this."

"Yes, Lena does," Lena said, shaking her head. "I hope that wasn't the big secret."

"No, he can *talk* talk!" Jin said, sounding frustrated. "Talk all by himself!"

"For a long time now," Rufus said. "Treats to celebrate Lena coming back?"

"Not right now, little man," Lena said, deciding to ignore Jin, as he was clearly going through something at the moment. And that was disappointing considering she'd half hoped Jin might be able to teleport them to the shadowlands, because then *The Tales of All Things* would have been wrong: they wouldn't have needed a guide, this Boy Who Was Freed. And if that part was wrong, maybe so was the rest? Maybe she didn't have anything to prove and could still save everyone?

But no, Jin was in no state to use magic. Not at the moment, anyway. If he tried it now, he might teleport them in the opposite direction, or to the glowing white rock the moon giant carried across the sky. And they didn't have time to wait for him to recover.

Which meant that at least so far, the fairy queens' story was coming true. The thought made Lena want to throw up.

At least she knew where to find the guide, thanks to Gwentell. They reached the knight's house a few moments later, and Lena reached out to open the door, only to find it locked. Without even thinking, she pulled back her arm, preparing to punch the door down.

But then the fairy queens' words came rushing back to her, and she froze. Breaking down a door was something a destructive creature would do. Yes, she didn't have the time to waste on unlocking it, and this almost certainly wasn't one of the trials, but wasn't she trying to show she could stay calm and not destroy things? That giants could be just as gentle as any other being?

Okay, try just this once to act more like a human. It can't be that hard. To open the door, humans would . . . humans would . . .

Actually, she had no idea *what* humans would do to get

through a locked door. Probably come back later? But that wasn't exactly an option.

She raised a hand, then knocked gently, trying not to damage the door at all. "Hello, may we come in?" she asked, trying to sound as polite as possible.

"Jill says the knight is gone," Jin pointed out.

"I know he is," Lena said, gritting her teeth to keep from yelling at him. "I'm just trying not to be such a giant about it all."

"Why?" Jin asked. "You *are* a giant about it all."

"I *know*, and it's because of that . . . Listen, just stop asking questions, okay?"

Jin nodded, then moved to her side and also knocked. "Hello, we may come in," he said, changing her question to a statement, just as she'd apparently ordered him to. He leaned in as if listening, then smiled. "The door says yes, we can!"

And then as Lena stared at him in confusion, Jin turned one of his fingers into a key shape, stuck it in the lock, and turned it. The lock clicked, and he turned the knob with his other hand, pushing the door open in front of her.

"Um, thank you?" she said, then quickly moved inside before he could talk about how fun the word "welcome" was.

Thomas's home had just been built in the last month, after

the attack by the Faceless, so everything still looked new and organized. The house's main room was cozy, with dark wooden walls and a fire crackling merrily in the fireplace.

While Thomas had previously kept his things in a secret cave in the mountain that led back to Lena's giant village, now an assortment of magical items covered various bookshelves and tables. A few swords hung on the walls next to a shield or two, all sized for humans, not Lilliputians, including one with a transparent blade, now cracked and broken.

"Jill's sword!" Jin said, pointing at it. "She says we need to take that with us, if we want her to come along."

"If 'Jill' is even real," Lena mumbled, glancing around.

"Jill is trying to punch you for that," Jin told her, giggling. "Miss miss miss. Oh, now she's punching me!"

"Good for her," Lena said, her anger rising. But even as she got more irritated with the genie, she forced herself to calm down. She wasn't going to let her anger take over, no matter how annoying Jin was. "I mean, that's so fun!"

"It is!" Jin agreed, still laughing.

Her jaw began to hurt from grinding her teeth together, so Lena took a deep breath, trying to relax. If she couldn't even overcome her giant impulses here in the Cursed City, then how was she going to beat the trials? What would she do when the shadow magic was all around her, trying to turn her against everyone she loved?

"We're supposed to find someone here," Lena told Jin, hoping to distract him, and therefore be less irritated by him. "A Boy Who Was Freed, according to the fairy queens."

"Freed of what?" Jin asked, and Lena shrugged, having no idea herself. Other than the fire going, there was no sign of anyone in the house. She quickly peeked into the knight's bedroom and found it empty as well. Frowning, she turned back to Jin. "Maybe we missed them?"

"I don't even know them, so I'm not sure I'd miss them yet," Jin said, as if he were worried about her mistaking his feelings for whoever this was.

"Maybe we should wait for them?" she asked, not really wanting an answer from Jin, but now at a loss. Without a guide, they wouldn't get far, and she had no idea how to find this Boy Who Was Freed if he wasn't in the knight's house.

Jin slowly looked around the room, then squealed with joy. "No need to wait, I found them!" he shouted, leaping forward to grab one of the bookshelves. He lifted it up with one hand, his muscles growing far too large for his arm, revealing a tiny but luxurious room, just big enough for Thomas outside his armor. It held a small bed, dresser, and washbasin, along with a trunk and some miniscule weapons on the wall.

And there, lying on the bed, was a six-inch-tall boy with brown hair, looking strangely familiar.

"Aha!" Jin shouted, reaching in to grab the surprised boy.

"Aha!" Lena shouted, this time actually agreeing with him.

"*Aha!*" shouted the boy, hanging by his shirt from Jin's grasp. "I knew thieves would be along to steal from the Last Knight. But unfortunately for you, he left me here to protect his things, and you've now fallen into my deadly trap." The tiny boy grinned in a weird, threatening way. "You now have just *five seconds* to leave before it springs, or you'll all be *doomed*!"

CHAPTER 14

in glanced at Lena, who crossed her arms and waited out the five seconds.

"I meant *ten* seconds!" the adorably handsome boy said, now facing away from them as he slowly spun around, dangling from Jin's fingers. "I'd run now if I were you!"

"Wait, I know you," Lena said, her face brightening. "You're the Faceless boy I captured!"

The boy snorted. "I've never been captured in my life. You must be mistaking me for some other Lilliputian."

She grabbed him and lifted him up to her eye level. "No, you're him," she said, squinting. "I'd seen your face before then. What's your name?"

"Of course you've seen my face," the boy said, glaring at her defiantly. "I am extremely important! My name is Prince

Golbasto Momarem Evlame Gurdilo Shefin Mully Ully Gue, heir to the emperor of Lilliput, scourge of the Big People, lethal to my enemies, and probably lethal to my friends, too, because I am in fact *just that dangerous*."

Jin let out a dreamy sigh. "You're *just that cute*, is more like it!" he said, and patted the boy on the head.

The boy reared back and snapped his teeth at Jin, which just made Jin's heart hurt from how adorable the Lilliputian was. "You'll lose that hand if you touch me again, Tall Boy!"

"*I'm* a genie!" Jin said brightly. "My name is Jin, and I'm not a prince or heir to anything!"

"*How* soon is this spell going to wear off, again?" Jill asked, sounding tired.

"Should be within a couple of hours," Jin told her, then paused to wonder how he'd known that.

"What should be?" the boy asked.

"Ignore him—he's under a spell and talking to invisible people," Lena said, making Jin grin widely at how correct she was. "So, Golbasto—"

"*You* may address me as Prince Shefin," the boy said, giving her a haughty look. "Or Your Majesty, lest I call my forces down upon you to teach you some manners."

Jin laughed out loud, just not able to take how cute this boy was. He wondered if the Lilliputian would mind living in Jin's pocket for the rest of his life, just popping up and acting all tough. Prince Shefin probably *would* mind, but it was worth asking, just in case.

Before Jin could, though, Lena gave the prince a disbelieving look. "Okay, um, *Your Majesty*," she said, narrowing her eyes. "Here's the thing: we need a guide through the shadowlands, and apparently you're supposed to be it. So I'm going to need you to—"

The Lilliputian laughed an obviously fake laugh, which Jin was extremely tempted to try out himself. "The shadowlands? You *must* be joking. I'd rather be hunted by rabid mongooses!"

"That can be arranged," Lena said, and Prince Shefin squealed as she tightened her grip. "The Last Knight is going to . . . He's in *danger*, and we're going to save him. Now you can either help us get to him first and *stop* the Golden King, or I can introduce you to my very hungry cat here." She nodded at Rufus, who Jin now realized had been staring at Shefin intently this whole time, making an odd chirping noise.

Shefin turned haughtily toward the giant cat, took a long look, and went extremely pale. "You don't scare me," he said, his voice cracking. "I've fought off a *dozen* cats that size before." He paused. "But I suppose I could listen to what you have to say, just in case, as I wouldn't want to hurt your pet. What's this about the Last Knight facing danger?"

"He's going to try to take over shadow magic!" Jin said helpfully. "But he won't be able to control it, and he'll get consumed by it, and spread darkness over the whooooole world." He shook his head sadly. "I just hope we have enough candles so we can still see!"

Shefin glanced back and forth between Jin and Lena. "Is he okay?" he asked her.

"Not even a little," she said. "He's under a fairy-queen spell."

"Ah," Shefin said, nodding knowingly. "I have no idea what those are."

"Doesn't matter," Lena said. "The Last Knight won't be able to resist the shadow, and will bring about the very thing he's trying to stop, unless *you* help us get to him first. Instead of trying to use it, we're going to imprison the shadow, then take down the Golden King when he doesn't have the magic to use anymore. But we need a guide to get through the shadowlands and find the Golden King, or we're all doomed."

"What you *need* is a teleporter," the Lilliputian boy said.

"Because there's no way you're getting through the shadow-lands alive."

"Oh, do you *have* a teleporter?" Lena asked, her face brightening, which made Jin extremely happy.

"Of course not," the boy said, rolling his eyes. "I gave mine to the Last Knight, so he could get back to Lilliput fast. I wanted to go with him and join in the revolution, which as the heir to Lilliput is not only my responsibility, but my privilege. Basically, I was *born* to help people by revolting. But Sir Thomas decided I was too important to risk, and ordered me to stay behind here." He smiled as if reminiscing. "My subjects all just love me so much! I can't imagine how devastated they'd be if I were hurt."

"So you're *not* here to protect all of the knight's things from thieves?" Lena said, raising an eyebrow.

"Obviously that, too," Shefin said, smiling smugly back at her. "I may be small, but I contain multitudes."

"I contain multitudes too!" Jin shouted, and changed his form to a bunch of his favorite human looks, from the redheaded girl to the enormous, bearded man he used when trying to intimidate other humans, and then to one of his favorites, the shape he just called Mr. Dragon—

"Okay, can we all just calm down?" Lena said, pointedly looking at Jin, who sadly left Mr. Dragon behind and resumed his usual boy form, which was probably for the best, as Rufus had taken one look at his dragon form and launched himself across the room. "You're right, Prince Shefin. I don't want to go through the shadowlands, and I *really* don't want to face the shadow magic."

"That's the first intelligent thing you've said today," Prince Shefin said, and then gasped as she squeezed her fist again.

"Jin has a spell that can transport us places," she said, glaring at the prince. "If you tell him where Lilliput is, then maybe *he* can take us. You know, once he's got his mind back."

The prince shook his head. "Can't be done. The Golden King had his shadow-controlling twins put up a magical barrier, and that keeps out everything except for Lilliputian technology, like our teleporters. He had to make an exception for those since that's what the Faceless use."

"How does *your* magic work, but his can't?" Lena said, nodding at Jin, who nodded back.

"Because it's *technology*," Shefin said, glaring at her. "Not just magic."

"Okay, sorry, so what is technology?"

Shefin shrugged. "Basically just magic." Lena growled, and he quickly continued before she could squeeze him again. "I mean, it *manipulates* magic. We don't have any magical power ourselves, so we've learned to control it using what we call Science." The smug smile returned. "You've probably never heard of it."

"I *really* don't like you," Lena said.

The prince gasped. "You dare insult the heir to the emperor of Lilliput? Guards! Arrest this girl!"

Lena and Jin both looked around for any Lilliputian guards. When none appeared, they both turned back to the prince.

"Okay, that was admittedly a long shot," he said with a sigh, then looked up at Lena sadly. "Is Sir Thomas truly in danger? You Big People have made it a habit to lie to my kind over the centuries, so forgive me if I don't believe you without proof."

"I could show you the fairies' *Tales of All Things* that explains all of this, but it's not in a language either of us could read," Lena told him, getting more irritated from the sound of it. "And honestly, we don't have time to prove it to you. So you can either help us voluntarily, or I'll just carry you in my fist into the shadowlands. Then it'll be up to you whether you want to help us through or get controlled by the shadow again."

The prince glared up at her. "There's no need for threats, large girl."

"It's *Lena*," she said through clenched teeth.

"Oh, I know who you are," the prince said. "The knight told me all about you. But he also warned me not to listen if anyone came here claiming he was in trouble." Lena started to say something, but he put up a hand to stop her. "Still, your grip here is beginning to really hurt, so let's just say I'm open to your ideas."

"Good," Lena said, then closed her eyes like she was upset about something. "I'm . . . I'm sorry. I shouldn't be acting like this. I need to be . . . more peaceful."

"Well I'm all for *that*," the Lilliputian said. "Does that mean you'll let me go?"

"Nice try."

"So 'peaceful' has a different meaning in Big People language, got it," the prince said, tapping his lip. "If I truly have no choice, then I will lead you to the Last Knight. However, if it turns out you are lying to me and mean him harm, I will do *everything* in my power to stop you, then make you suffer for your betrayal, even if it takes me—"

Lena knelt down and slid the adorable prince across the

floor into the room he'd been hiding in. "Get your stuff—we're leaving as soon as you're ready."

"How *dare* you treat me like this?" the prince said, picking himself up indignantly and dusting his clothes off. But one look from Lena sent him back into his room, muttering under his breath.

As he gathered up his belongings, Lena grabbed Jin's arm and pulled him to the other side of the room. "Let's keep your thoughts about the Last Knight being evil to yourself, okay?" she whispered, quiet enough so that the Lilliputian couldn't hear. "We can't let him know that we're going to have to stop Thomas, no matter what it takes."

"Right!" Jin said, apparently too loudly, as her eyes widened. "Right!" he said again, more quietly.

Lena glanced over at the boy, who was folding a bunch of very expensive-looking clothes. "I also want to ask a favor," she said, turning back to Jin with a worried expression. "You're not going to believe this, but I really did see this boy before, back before the Faceless attack." She sighed deeply, and her face began to turn red. "This ridiculous mirror in my family's house claimed that I was going to meet my true love, and then showed me *his* picture."

Jin's mouth dropped almost to his chest, until he remembered it wasn't supposed to do that and quickly pushed it back up. "Your . . . true love?"

Lena's eyes widened. "Um, I've never seen a chin do that before. But yeah, that's what it said. But it was obviously wrong, because I'm not going to fall in love with him. There's no chance. I've never felt that way for anyone, and I'm not going to start now."

Jin felt a weird sort of weight on his chest, and he swallowed hard, trying to process all that information at once. Some magical mirror claimed Shefin was Lena's true love? But she didn't feel that way about anyone?

Not even Jin?

"Maybe you'll change your mind?" he said. "Not about Shefin, but someone different, someone who you know better, and—"

She snorted. "No, it's just who I am. Trust me. I have zero interest in people that way. But I'm worried the mirror meant *he* was going to fall in love with *me*, and that could lead to problems, since we need him to guide us to Lilliput. So help me keep an eye out, and make sure he doesn't suddenly start having feelings for me or something. That'd be *very* awkward."

Jin's eyes narrowed, and he glared at the handsome boy. "*Very* awkward," he repeated, wondering how the Lilliputian would enjoy a trip to meet the sun giant. "Awkward, awkward, *awkward.*"

And for once, he didn't find the word "awkward" fun at *all*.

CHAPTER 15

Lena let out a sigh of relief, thankful that Jin hadn't made fun of her about the whole "true love" ridiculousness. There were too many prophecies going on right now, and she honestly couldn't handle the mirror's on top of everything else.

"Almost ready?" she called out to Shefin, as Jin glared at the boy. Maybe she should have waited until the fairy queens' spell had worn off before asking for his help.

"Oh, I'm sorry. Did you want me to leave behind the only protection we'll have from the shadow magic?" the prince asked, stopping his packing. "Is that what you wanted? Or did you want to be quiet, and trust that I know what I'm doing?"

The urge to stamp him into the ground suddenly felt overwhelming, only for that urge to immediately turn to shame as she realized what she was thinking. Crushing random tiny people was probably not going to help her argument that giants weren't inherently bad people.

"Take your time," she said, then slumped into one of the knight's human-sized chairs to wait, wondering if it was already too late to prove the fairy queens' story wrong.

"Jill says I *really* need to take her sword," Jin pointed out, and moved toward the broken, translucent sword hanging on the wall. "According to her, 'We're not getting anywhere without someone with half a brain along.' And she claims she's got a full brain, so that works!"

Lena laughed in spite of herself, only to leap to her feet as the Lilliputian prince came sprinting out of his hole, holding what looked like a needle. "Stop!" he shouted, aiming his "weapon" at Jin.

Jin froze, then turned toward the tiny boy, radiating anger. "Don't tell me what to do, *Your Majesty*," he growled.

"That's exactly what My Majesty does, tell people what to do," Shefin said, and whipped the needle through the air. "I told you: I'm here to protect the knight's belongings from any thieves. You will *leave* that sword where it is, genie, or I shall become extremely *vexed*."

"Vexed means 'annoyed, frustrated, or worried'!" Jin shouted back, then grabbed for the sword on the wall.

The Lilliputian boy growled, then swung out with his needle. As he did, the tiny blade increased in size, shooting toward Jin faster than Lena could see. The needle stabbed into Jin's shoulder and continued right through it, making Lena gasp.

But Jin just glanced down at his shoulder, turned insubstantial, then shrugged himself out of the needle's path. He turned back toward Shefin holding this Jill person's broken sword, and aimed it now at the little prince. "Nice try, but I'm completely empty inside!"

"You and me both," the prince sneered, and slowly circled around. Jin matched him, and Lena had to fight the urge to punch both of them.

"Enough!" she shouted. "Jin, are you sure we need this Jill woman along with us? I can't even see her."

"Jill says that sounds like a personal problem, and yes, we need her," he said. "The twins who control the shadow magic are her niece and nephew."

The prince's eyes widened. "*That* Jill? Sister-in-law to Princess May?"

Jin tilted his head like he was listening. "Jill says May is *her* sister-in-law, not the other way around." He paused. "I don't know what that means."

"It means we're wasting time!" Lena shouted. "Shefin, do you have everything you need?"

"I have enough," he said. "But I cannot allow this genie to remove the knight's sword."

"*Jill's* sword," Jin said. "And we need her! She says that the sword of the Eyes has a connection to anyone who wields it, and that connection is what's allowed her spirit to escape from the golden statue the king made out of her. But she can't go too far without it, so if we want her help, we'll need to take it with us." He sighed. "Whoa, that was a lot to pass along. Oh, and she says, 'You're welcome for not insulting anyone this time.'"

Fair enough. "All right, here's a compromise," Lena said. "*I will take the sword and put it in my pouch. That way it's along with us, but no one can use it. And then when we, ah, *rescue* the Last Knight, we'll give it back. Okay?"

"Never!" Prince Shefin said.

"Jill says she'd rather be turned into *another* statue than let you give it back—"

"Good, I'm glad you both agree," Lena said, and grabbed the sword from Jin's hand. As she did, the blade began to cloud up with an odd black color, so she nervously shoved it into her infinitely large pouch before it did anything strange, then cinched the pouch shut. "There. Now we can bring the Invisible Cloud of Hate with us, because what could be more of a help?"

Jin nodded. "Thank you, Lena. And Jill says she likes your snark, even if it's been turned against her unfairly."

Lena saluted in the general direction she thought the invisible woman might be, then turned to Shefin. "Now, what was that you were saying about a way to protect us from the shadow?"

The prince gave her an annoyed look. "First, let's discuss who is actually in charge of this mission, since apparently there's an urgent need. Anyone who's royalty, raise their hands."

Shefin's hand shot into the air, followed by Jin. "*You're* royalty?" Lena asked him in surprise.

"No, but I don't like him," Jin whispered loudly to her.

"As the *sole* royal here," Shefin continued, glaring at Jin, "it is up to me to lead the rest of you. Now, put that sword back. That is an *order*."

Lena dug her fingernails into her hand to keep from smushing him into a pancake. "Tell you what," she said, and grabbed him again before he could dodge away. "How about I put *you* in my pouch, and you can hold the sword all you want.

I don't really remember what else is in there, though, so watch out for anything that might want to eat you."

Before he could object, she loosened her pouch, then held him up over it, ready to drop him.

"Ah, well, yes," he said quickly, eying the pouch nervously. "Perhaps you two can be my advisors, and I will give my word that I'll take your opinions into account with every decision?"

"Have fun!" Lena said, and started lowering him in.

"Okay, okay!" he shouted, kicking out at the pouch. "Don't put me in there. You can be in charge, you evil giant!"

"You *what?*" Lena asked, her eyes lighting up with anger. Smushing was too good for him now. Drop-kicking the Lilliputian into the fire seemed like a lot more fun.

"You *wonderful* giant," Shefin said quickly. "You probably misheard me the first time. Now, shall we be off?"

"That's what I thought," Lena said, and put Shefin up on her shoulder. At least that way the boy was close at hand, either for leading them or squishing, whichever made the most sense at the time. "Now, the shadow magic protection. What is it, and how does it work?"

"Oh, it's so easy to use that even you two should be able to understand it," Shefin said, settling himself on her tunic. "Ugh,

I've never felt such rough fabric. Anyway, the item creates and manipulates a large bubble of protective magic that will keep the shadow out, and all it takes is a positive attitude."

"A positive what?" Lena asked, raising an eyebrow. "You mean, like, we have to be optimistic?"

"Well, *slightly* more than that," he said with a shrug. "You have to think of something truly happy to make the magic work. If your mood changes even for a second and you lose that happy feeling, the magic instantly disappears, and the shadow will overwhelm us all." He smiled. "See? Easy!"

CHAPTER 16

h, you've got to be kidding me!" Jill shouted. "That's Pan's magic!"

"Jill says there's a pan in the magic," Jin said, pleased with himself for accurately passing along her message.

Lena ignored him to argue with the awful boy on her shoulder. "You're joking. If we stop thinking happy thoughts for even a second, we're going to get taken over by shadow magic? *That's* your protective spell?"

"I never said it was a spell," Shefin said, removing what appeared to be a human-sized ring from around his waist by shimmying it down his legs and stepping out of it. "We've created a way to store magic within this hoop, which coincidentally makes for some fine fashion—HEY!"

Lena ripped the ring from his hands and turned it over in her palm. "I don't like this at *all*. We're trying to save the world from overwhelming darkness. How are we supposed to think happy thoughts with that going on? Not to mention the tri . . ." She trailed off.

A hand waved in front of Jin, and he jumped back in surprise, having been focused on Lena. "Hey, this is the perfect job for you!" Jill said. "Take the ring, Jin. In your current mindless state, you'll be able to think happy thoughts for days. Just daydream about Lena!"

"Lena?" he said, and the giant girl looked over at him. "Jill says I should take the ring, because I'm mindless and can daydream about . . . people."

Lena blinked. "You know, that's not the worst idea. But what happens if the fairy queens' spell wears off while you're using the ring?"

"I'm *always* happy," Shefin said, glaring at them all. "I'm also the one with the most experience with the ring, so if you *don't* mind, I'd like it back!"

"Not going to happen," Lena said absently. She moved closer to Jin and handed him the ring. "You can do this, right?"

He grinned at the sudden joy he felt over her asking him to

do such an important task. Honestly, he felt like he could fly, even without magic. "If you think I can, then I can be as happy as you think I can be! Which is *so* happy!"

She winced, then smiled again. "Yeah, that! Okay. We better move quickly." She pulled her head back to look at Shefin. "Which way do we go to Lilliput?"

"Oh, so we're going to walk?" he asked, then pointed in the direction of the front door. "Well, it's that way, and should only take you a couple of weeks. Now, if you put *me* back in charge, as I was born to be, then perhaps I can share some of our technology that might carry us there faster."

"Faster than Seven League Boots?" Lena asked, nodding at Rufus.

Shefin turned to glance at the cat. "Oh, is that what those are? I hadn't seen some in person before. . . . Why is this creature staring at me like that?"

"He wants to eat you," Jin told him, the thought playing out in his mind making him even happier. "Lena, can we let him?"

"Yes, Lena, we let him?" Rufus asked, making Shefin shudder nervously.

"He can *talk*, too?" the prince asked, losing some of his annoying confidence.

"And hunt," Jin said, delighting in all of this. "He's *so* good at hunting. Especially mice. Mouses? Mice."

Lena just shook her head as she opened the front door, then climbed up onto Rufus's back. "No eating anyone, little man," she said to the cat. "Jin, get up here. We need to get going."

Jin floated up as well to sit behind her, with Jill hovering next to him. "Who is the pan of magic?" he whispered to her as Rufus strode out the door.

"He's this satyr, a person with goat legs," Jill told him. "Used to kidnap children and bring them to the Land of Never, where they thought time stood still, and they'd never have to grow up. Turns out that was all in their minds, and they *did* get older, just without knowing it. But Pan's magic only worked on people who were happy, so he needed to trick them into thinking they were having the time of their lives."

Jin tried to imagine that but couldn't get past the fact that a frying pan was doing all of this. "Weird," he said as they passed through the empty streets of the Cursed City.

"More than you know," Jill said. "But what's worse is that I handed Pan over to the Wicked Queen, when the Last Knight was still in charge of her Eyes. Pan disappeared after everything, so Thomas must have taken him for . . . whatever magic the

Lilliputians needed. Just more proof that Thomas was never a good guy."

"Okay, Rufus," Lena said as they reached the front gate. "I need you to use your boots and jump in just a moment. But first, we need to know how far the shadowlands are." She turned to look at Shefin.

He stared back at her. "What, in Lilliputian terms? It's probably around ten billion Mildenos. Does that answer your question?"

"Tell her it's over three leagues," Jill said to Jin. "But err on the shorter side. We do *not* want to dive into the shadow without being ready."

"Jill says it's three leagues, but dive into the shorter side," Jin passed along, making Jill groan.

"The spell must be fading, because I almost understood that," Lena said. "We should definitely hurry, then!"

She whispered into Rufus's ear, and he leapt forward, the surrounding countryside whooshing away in an instant. They landed a moment later just outside a deep, dark, shadow-filled forest.

Lena's whole body went rigid as she stared into the darkness, then jumped when Jin tapped her shoulder. "Are you okay?" he asked, his mood plummeting with his concern for her.

"I'm fine," she said, her eyes locked on the darkness inside the woods. "Is . . . is this it? Is this the start of the shadow-lands? Because I only told Rufus to jump *two* leagues, not three."

"The Golden King is spreading the shadow across the land, just like the Last Knight said," Jill said. "It won't be long now until it reaches the Cursed City. But we're not quite at its start, as it's still a little ways away in the forest. You can probably feel it now, though."

Jin frowned and reached out with his magical senses, trying to find the shadow that way. He could feel *something* angry, not too far away, but it didn't necessarily feel evil, like he assumed the shadows would. Instead, it almost felt . . . familiar.

"Jin, you should put the ring on," Lena said to him. "We should make sure we're protected before we go in, so we're not taken by surprise."

"Oh, the shadow doesn't need surprise," Shefin said, his voice sounding much less energetic than usual. Jin glanced up at the horrible Lilliputian and saw he didn't look any more thrilled than Lena did about being so close to the woods. "It takes *everything*, and doesn't let you go. The only reason I got out was because of Sir Thomas. Otherwise, I'd still be stuck under its control."

"Because of Lena, too," Jin pointed out. "She's the one who captured you."

Shefin seemed to consider this, then nodded. "He's got a point, which is new. I owe you as well, Lady Giant. And when we have taken Lilliput back, I will reward you with riches beyond your wildest dreams."

Jin narrowed his eyes, not liking where this was going. Lena seemed to think the same, as she quickly shrugged, almost knocking Shefin off her shoulder.

"Yeah, there's no need for that," she said. "Anyone would have done it. And it was random that it was you. Certainly no prophecy or anything like that!"

The Lilliputian just stared up at her thoughtfully, which made Jin even more nervous. He had to change the subject, and quickly. "Okay! Time to protect us. I'll think happy thoughts, and we'll be ready to go." With that, he put the ring on his finger and imagined Shefin screaming and running from a very hungry Rufus.

The thought brought him *great* joy, and immediately a green sphere of light appeared around them, just wide enough to cover Rufus's whole body.

"Not bad," Shefin said, leaning over to examine the sphere. "It appears to be stable. But if the genie thinks bad thoughts—"

"Don't worry," Jin told him, smiling with all of his teeth. "I've got all kinds of fun daydreams to go through. I'll keep us all safe!"

Lena reached back and touched his arm. "Thank you, Jin. Our lives are in your hands."

The green sphere doubled in brightness, and Jin smiled back at her.

"Fantastic," Jill said, snorting. "All of our lives depend on a genie's crush on a giant girl. What could possibly go wrong with that?" She sighed. "We're all going to die, aren't we?"

CHAPTER 17

At Lena's urging, a trembling Rufus slowly walked them into the woods. She scratched his neck to try to reassure him but wasn't sure how effective that'd be, considering she was shaking herself.

They hadn't even gotten to the shadow yet, and already she was terrified to face it, even with the protective Lilliputian magic. The fairy queens and Thomas both seemed convinced her giant heritage would mean it could control her easily, and she was terrified to see if they were right.

But it wasn't just the shadow, either. The Trials of Wrath, Warfare, and Wickedness would take place somewhere in these darkened lands. But she still didn't really understand what the trials would be, or how they might test her. What sort of challenge would she face to have to overcome anger or choose not to fight? And then there was the Trial of Wickedness, which she didn't even fully understand. Would it just require not being evil?

One of Rufus's boots snapped a twig, bringing Lena's attention back to the present, and she shook her head, trying to stay calm, stay focused. She couldn't afford to be lost in thought while approaching the shadow. Even the regular, everyday shadows grew darker the farther Rufus padded into the forest. The trees and dirt path they followed took on a greenish tinge from Shefin's ring, and the eerie light didn't exactly help Lena's mood, but at least she knew it was there and keeping shadow magic out. That was the important thing, as without it, they had no prayer of making it through, worthy or not.

"I do not like this, Lena," Rufus said softly, his whiskers twitching. "The dark gives me bad tingles."

"Jill says that's normal," Jin said. "That we should all be feeling the bad tingles by now, or there's something wrong with us."

"Does he always make this much sense?" Shefin whispered to Lena, and she almost laughed.

"Stop, he's getting better," she said.

"And also, he can *hear* you," Jin added, and the green light shimmered a bit, growing dimmer.

"Jin, watch what you're thinking!" Lena shouted, only for the light to get even fainter. "I mean, you're doing *so* great at this! You're really the perfect person to protect us all."

The light brightened once more, and she let out a sigh of relief.

"Jill says that trick isn't going to work forever!" Jin said happily behind her. "*She* thinks we're doomed. I think we're doing great, myself!"

Before Lena could respond to *that*, something caught her attention, movement out of the corner of her eye. She immediately turned to look but saw nothing but more darkness beyond the light of the magical sphere.

"We're in it now," Shefin said quietly. "Shadow magic hides within the natural darkness, and will probe our shield until it finds a weakness."

Well, *that* wasn't a happy thought. Lena's heart began racing, and she took a deep breath to again calm herself, but it didn't help. Just outside the thin protective bubble of magic lay the evil that had created her kind, waiting to pull her in, take her over, and unleash all the power and strength she had on the world if she let it.

But she wouldn't let it. She *couldn't*.

Another quick movement caught Lena's attention, and again she whirled around to catch it, but whatever it was had disappeared by the time she looked.

"What sort of weaknesses is it looking for?" she whispered to Shefin. "Does the sphere have any kind of opening in it?"

"No, I meant more that it's trying to *create* weaknesses in the shield," he said. "The more afraid we are, the more likely it is that the protective sphere will fail." He must have noticed her fear, as he smiled. "But don't worry. Lilliputian science can *easily*—"

A large black shape slammed into the magical sphere from the side, knocking Rufus from the path, and sending his riders tumbling from his back. Lena landed hard, slamming a shoulder into a nearby tree, and for a moment she couldn't think, couldn't understand what had just happened.

Then she felt something cold on her hand and turned to find it lying outside the green light of the magical sphere. Dark tendrils of shadow magic had already begun to infect her, turning her fingers pale and lifeless.

"*No!*" she screamed, and yanked her hand back inside the green light as quickly as she could. As her fingers passed through the light, the shadow dissolved out of them, leaving a terrible, acrid smoke behind.

And beyond the light, the shadow hissed as if it were in pain.

"How did it *do* that?" she demanded of Shefin, who'd managed to land safely on Rufus's back. "How did it knock us off the path like that? I thought it didn't have any physical form!"

"Oh, it can take one, when it wants," Shefin said, wincing a bit as he stood up. He looked smaller somehow than he had in the knight's house, and far paler. All traces of confidence had disappeared from his voice too. "*Any* form," he continued, his voice even softer now. "And that makes it so much worse."

"There's *worse*?" Lena demanded, picking him up and putting him back on her shoulder. As she did, the sphere shimmered, getting dimmer, and she immediately looked around for Jin, finding him just inside the shield. "Jin, are you okay?"

The genie looked slightly dazed, though he didn't appear to be hurt. It was more like he was staring off into the shadow with a strange sort of curiosity. "It's so *angry*," he said, nodding into the darkness. "And it wants something. No, some*one*. One of us."

Lena's eyes widened, and she followed his gaze into the shadow, which was now pushing up the sides of the sphere, trying to hold them in place. The light dimmed again, and

Lena desperately wished she could punch something. "Jin, you *have* to concentrate! Happy thoughts!"

"We can all help," Shefin said, and nodded down at the genie. Lena carried him to Jin's side, and the Lilliputian leapt down to put a hand on Jin's finger, the one with the magical ring. "We're going to destroy the Golden King, and free everyone from shadow magic," Shefin said quietly, closing his eyes. "And it's going to feel *so good* to be able to just live freely again!"

The light brightened once more, but the shadow pushed back, squeezing in on the sphere from all sides, terrifying Lena that it might collapse the protective magic. She dropped to Jin's side herself, and put her own hand on top of Shefin's, trying her best to think of something happy, anything at all.

Mrs. Hubbard welcoming me to the Cursed City.

The Cursed City, which no longer trusted her and hated her kind.

The first time the Last Knight showed me his true self.

The Last Knight who believed giants were created by evil.

This wasn't *working*, and the sphere was definitely bending in places now as the shadow's tentacles crushed the light beneath their grasp, like some kind of giant squid.

"Lena, we need your *help* here!" Shefin shouted as the light dimmed again.

"Jill says we're in *huge* trouble," Jin pointed out. "She says she wishes she hadn't come along now."

"See?" Shefin said. "I was right! We should have left the knight's sword where it was, you thieves!"

"Enough!" Lena shouted, the light beginning to fade in places now, almost to the point of disappearing. "We can't fight each other, or we'll definitely get devoured by the shadow! Now, everyone focus on your happiest thought!"

Jin glanced over at her, and his worries seemed to melt away as a dreamy sort of smile appeared on his face. The fading spots abruptly surged back, but the shadow doubled its efforts, compressing the sphere even farther.

"I'm going to lead the revolution against the Golden King and become emperor of Lilliput, a free land once more," Shefin whispered to himself, his eyes closed. "And I will rule my people with an *iron fist*!"

Lena blinked at that, but this was no time to judge. She needed a happy thought, *something* she could use that wasn't tainted by the shadow magic itself.

Lena the Giant, Creel the Sparktender had called her.

But wasn't Creel just as much a product of evil as she was?

Her mother and father hugging her tightly, careful not to harm their tiny child . . .

A wave of warmth flowed through Lena, and somehow she could feel the magic around them strengthen.

"It's working!" Jin shouted. "Aw, I'm so *happy*!"

Lena opened her eyes just in time to watch the green light shine brightly like the sun giant's fireball. The shadow beyond it flinched away, then slunk off into the darkness of the woods, leaving them safe, at least for the moment.

"Well," Shefin said, taking his hand off the ring on Jin's finger. "That went better than I expected, honestly."

"What?" Lena shouted. "The shadow could have broken through! We were almost taken over!"

Shefin nodded. "That's what I just said. Did you really think this was going to be easy? Odds are, none of us make it to Lilliput, because the shadow will be back, and now it's *angry*." He smiled slightly. "Might I suggest we get a move on, then?"

CHAPTER 18

ell, *that* was fun," Jill said, shuddering, as Lena picked Shefin up and put him back on her shoulder, then climbed up onto Rufus's back again. Jin followed right behind, trying to ignore Shefin and focus on how amazing Lena was. "Tiny boy is right: there's no way we're getting through the shadowlands at this rate."

"It's not all like this," Jin told her. "There's a protected city not too far from here, and then a farming community, and a goblin village as well. So three spots we can stop to rest."

Lena turned to look back over her shoulder at him, and Shefin had to grab onto her tunic to keep from falling off. "Wait, what was that?" she said, looking at him anxiously. "Three what?"

"He's *oddly* correct," Shefin said, frowning. "At least about that first one. There *is* a city up ahead that holds protection from the shadows somehow. At least, so I've heard."

"City?" Jill said. "What kind of horrifying city would exist in the middle of the shadowlands?" She frowned. "And how did *you* know about it, genie?"

Jin shrugged, happy that everyone was so impressed with him suddenly. Why weren't they *always* treating him like this, when he had proven how smart he was over and over? "I must have picked it up somewhere," he said. "Come on, big cat, it won't take long if you actually run a bit!"

"Maybe genie should run with people on *his* back," Rufus said, growling slightly. Lena reached out to comfort him, and Jin felt a pang of jealousy but immediately pushed it away as the light of the protective sphere dimmed.

"The faster the better," Shefin said, eyeing the shield as well. "You people have too much angst for my comfort."

"Three safe spots, three trials," Lena whispered, but seeing Jin raise an eyebrow, she shook her head. "It's nothing—just something the fairy queens said. Forget it. Let's go."

At Lena's urging, Rufus began walking, then trotting, jostling them a bit more than Jin was used to on his back. Probably a combination of the rough terrain and the fact that with the shadow all around them now, it wasn't easy to see the path ahead, even for the cat's night vision, Jin guessed. Seeing through shadow magic wasn't like navigating in the dark. If nothing else, the shadows were *solid*.

"Aren't you just full of surprises today," Jill said, settling in to float at Jin's side.

He grinned, then reached out with his mind to her, hoping to speak in private. *Do you know what Lena meant, talking about three trials?*

Jill's eyes widened. "Another new trick. Did you always know how to do that?"

Jin stopped to think. How *did* he know how to do this? It'd just occurred to him that he could, so the others wouldn't keep getting confused by half a conversation. *I don't know, but it's not that hard.*

"Don't brag, it's annoying," Jill said, shaking her head. "Anyway, back to your question. The fairy queens probably told her about some prophecy or another. They've got this magic book called *The Tales of All Things*. My brother and sister-in-law used to think that was so funny, that fairies had a book of tales for some reason, but it was some awful inside joke, I think."

Good to know, Jin thought. *So what kind of trials would they be? I'm going to help Lena with them, but she doesn't seem to want to talk about it.*

"How would I know?" Jill asked, wincing as one of the shadows at their side whacked the sphere again. The shield seemed to hold better, now that Jin knew to expect it, and the attack only managed to rock Rufus slightly. "I was just guessing. But they do seem to like putting people through challenges, to make sure they fit the hero role the fairy queens love so much." Jill went silent for a moment, as if lost in thought.

Well, I'm going to need more than that if I'm going to help her through them.

"I think the point is that she has to do them on her own, genie boy," Jill said. "But I wouldn't worry. Lena's tough—she can handle this."

Do you think one might be about . . . Shefin? And how he's supposed to be her true love?

Jill groaned loudly. "Ugh, of course you'd think that, because you're stuck in one of these awful love triangle things. Knowing the fairy queens, I wouldn't be surprised if it was. They're all about setting people up." She cringed. "You people spend way too much time on all of that. Think of how much you could get done if you just didn't bother with love!"

The very thought made Jin a bit sad, which meant he had to immediately switch his thoughts back to Lena. Unfortunately, the fairy queens' spell seemed to be almost completely gone, so it wasn't quite so easy to stay focused on happy thoughts.

The shadows around them apparently picked up on that, as the attacks on the sphere began coming faster, more frequently.

"Um, are we almost there yet?" Lena asked, leaning down to hug Rufus's neck as he trotted along as best he could.

"From what I've heard, we should have been able to see the city by now, if not for the shadow," Shefin told her, making Jin roll his eyes.

"Actually, we wouldn't, because it's behind a *hill*," he told the Lilliputian, feeling a brief sense of satisfaction that managed to strengthen the sphere, just as another shadow struck it. "Surprised you didn't know that."

"Either way, I just want to *get* there already," Lena said, and whispered something in Rufus's ear. The cat began moving faster, which made for an even rougher ride as he tripped and stumbled on some surprise branches and rocks in the middle of the path.

The attacks sped up even more, like the shadow was sensing they might escape it. Jin could sense its rage over not managing to catch them . . . and something else, almost a fear of the three of them.

No, not the three. Just one.

The shadow doesn't want us all, he thought to Jill, not entirely understanding how he knew.

"Who's the lucky person?" Jill asked as they climbed a hill now, which meant they must be almost there. "My guess is the Lilliputian, since he was under the shadow's control before."

Maybe, Jin said, not sure either way. The fear was too vague, and he couldn't sense its source. Part of him wondered what would happen if he tried to communicate with the shadow, just like he was with Jill. Could he convince it they weren't a threat to the darkness?

Or would it just take him over through the mental connection?

"There!" Lena shouted, and the smallest pinprick of light appeared as they topped the hill. "I see it!"

But just as Lena's burst of hope spread to Jin, strengthening the magical sphere, an enormous hand reached out of the darkness and slammed into the protective spell, crashing them to a halt.

"Hello, little genie," said a voice of pure darkness. Jin looked up, and up, and *up* to find a sleek black dragon filling the forest path before them, one enormous paw holding their sphere in place. "You managed to escape from my magic mirror, I see. This time when I trap you, it will be *forever*."

"Uh-oh," Jill said quietly. "Remember how I said a rogue fairy queen trapped the ifrit in the magic mirror the first time? Well, this is her. Meet Malevolent."

CHAPTER 19

The dragon towered over the sphere, lit in the eerie green light of the protective spell. Real or not, the shadowy figure sent fear snaking through Lena's heart. But even worse, it wasn't alone. A rumble sent the ground beneath them shaking as an enormous face pushed through the trees, a face of a giant. And while it was too large, too close to make out the features, its voice was *instantly* recognizable. "Oh, *Lena*," her mother said, sounding disgusted.

"*Mom?*" Lena said, her voice cracking. "What are you . . . how can you *be* here?"

"I've come to take you home, Lena," her mother said, shaking her head and sending trees flying. "You truly thought you could resist the shadow? It's already inside you, my love. We were created from the darkness, and that's all we'll ever be. How can you not see that?"

Lena's eyes widened, and a strange roaring filled her ears, like she was about to faint. As if from a distance, Lena could hear the dragon shouting something at Jin, who didn't respond. The dragon roared, then sent shadowy black flames straight at the protective sphere, so hot Lena could feel them through the magic of the Lilliputian ring.

But that didn't matter. Nothing did but her mother's words.

"Why didn't you ever tell me?" Lena whispered, tears flowing freely now. "I was so *proud* of being a giant! I even got my epithet. But it's all gone so *wrong* since then!"

"That's just who we are, Lena," her mother said, slowly smiling. "Listen to your heart. Do you feel it? The urge deep inside to just *rip* this world apart?" A second rumbling came from deeper in the forest, and her mother's hand came exploding out, holding multiple trees in her grasp. "It just feels so *good* to destroy, doesn't it? That's thanks to the shadow, Lena. Embrace it! Become the giant you were always meant to be." And with that, she crushed the trees in her hand, sending wood flying in all directions.

Some of the debris struck the sphere, but Lena barely noticed, still too shocked by her mother's words. It took a furry headbutt to somehow break through her shock, and she looked down to find Rufus staring up at her with big, loving eyes. "Lena's mother talks lies," he whispered, purring quietly. "Scary lies. Scared, scared." He shivered, shaking his fur. "Lena does *not* listen."

"Oh, Shefin," said a voice from the other side of the sphere, another *familiar* voice, one that shouldn't have been anywhere near here. Lena slowly turned to find the Last Knight, his armor now tarnished and black, glaring down at the Lilliputian boy on Rufus's back, who must have fallen off Lena's shoulder when the dragon stopped their shield. "You think you can actually help the revolution? I hid you away in the Cursed City because you're far too *small*, even for a Lilliputian. You'd be useless in our fight against the Golden King!"

"But . . . I *want* to help!" Shefin said, his shoulders slumping defeatedly. "Please, give me a chance, Sir Thomas. I can be useful! I *need* to help the revolution. They're my people!"

"Are you not listening to me, Lena?" her mother asked, and slammed a fist against the ground, throwing them all into the air, including the sphere. The hit knocked Lena the rest of the way out of whatever hypnotic daze she'd been in, and she managed to catch Shefin on the way back down, before they hit the ground. She, Jin, and Rufus crashed to the forest floor hard, but at least the prince was protected in her grasp.

"This is the *worse* I mentioned before," the Lilliputian boy told her, his eyes wide. "The shadow is using our own fears against us. We can't listen to them, or we'll be lost!"

"Oh, there's no need to listen," the dragon said, and put her paw up against the sphere again. She slowly closed her claws into the green light, and one by one, they began to slide right through. Lena gasped, not able to believe it. The shadow before had been burned off by touching the Lilliputian magic, but now with the shield wavering, it must have the power to resist it. "We're not here to *convince* you. We're here to tell you what you already know, that everything you fear *will* come true."

A sword sliced through the green light just to Lena's right, and she whirled around to find the Last Knight standing with his weapon still piercing the sphere. "This is the real reason I left you all behind," he said, his voice low and disgusted. "The giant girl is a *monster*, and the genie's beyond useless. But you, boy, aren't even worth a second thought."

A giant hand pushed down on the sphere from above,

crushing the shield, and forcing it farther down into the dirt with each passing moment. "You want to fight back, don't you, Lena?" her mother said. "You want to punch and kick and *hurt* something, because that's who you are. That's who all giants are, dear. We revel in destruction, and fight to show our might! Embrace the shadow, my dear, because that's who you're meant to be. That's who you *already are*."

Lena shook her head frantically, not able to listen anymore. She tossed Shefin over to Rufus as she stood back up, then braced her shoulders against the green light, pushing back against her shadowy mother.

But the fake giant was far too strong, and the sphere started to deform into an oval, collapsing in on them the more the giant pushed.

"You can't win this way, Lena," her mother whispered. "Not by protecting them. *Fight* me. Come out here and show me the shadow inside of you. You'll be so much happier when you realize you're just as evil as the rest of us."

"The mirror was only the beginning, genie," the dragon said, her claws reaching out toward the somehow still-silent Jin. "This time, I'll trap you in an even tinier space, and for all eternity!"

"Your people think you're so pathetic," the Last Knight said to Shefin, who backed away from the shadowy Thomas, only to stumble and fall off Rufus's back. He landed hard, then fell to his knees, groaning. "I'm surprised the Golden King even used you as a Faceless. No wonder Lena was able to capture you so easily."

And then all the sadness, the hate, the *fear* was just too much, and the fading green sphere winked out for the briefest of moments. It reappeared just in time to stop Lena's mother from crushing them completely, but it wouldn't be long now. The shadow would break through, and they'd all be taken over by it. There was nothing they could do.

The fairy queens had told Lena to overcome her giant self, to ignore her instincts to fight. But resisting the urge didn't seem to even slow the shadow down.

But what other choice did she have? The shadow clearly wanted her to fight it, and to give in to that temptation was to lose herself in the darkness. She couldn't face it, not like she wanted to; all she had was her muscles now, and even those weren't going to be enough to protect her friends.

Her mother's overwhelming strength sent Lena to her knees, and she whimpered in pain and terror. Why was she even bothering now? They'd already lost; it was just a matter of time. There was nothing they could do, *nothing*—

Something pawed at her back, meowing softly. "Lena is *good*," Rufus said quietly. "Lena takes care of me. Lena is *not* bad, like mother says."

She looked down sadly at her pet, not sure what to even say. The shadow was going to take Rufus, as well, and she'd do anything to stop that. He didn't deserve this. Neither did Jin or Shefin.

And maybe she could still save them.

"Jin, get on Rufus," she growled, barely able to hold the sphere up against her mother's crushing hand now. "Take Shefin, too."

"What are you going to do?" the Lilliputian boy asked as Jin grabbed him and floated up on her cat's back once again.

"I'm going to throw you as hard as I can in the direction that we saw the light," Lena told them, her face now wet with both sweat and tears. "It's your only chance. If I can do it fast enough, the shadow might not be able to capture you."

Jin and Shefin looked at each other, and Jin dropped the Lilliputian roughly onto Rufus's back, then dismounted. "Nope," the genie said. "That's not going to happen. If anyone's sacrificing themselves—" He paused, looking past her for a moment. "*You*, be quiet." He turned back to Lena, continuing as if not interrupted by the Invisible Cloud of Hate. "If *anyone's* sacrificing themselves, it's going to be me. The shadow can't actually hurt me."

"Yes, it *can*!" Lena groaned, her muscles shrieking in pain. "The Faceless's swords hurt you, and they probably had shadow magic in them!"

"Not exactly," Shefin said, standing up to say something else, but Jin flicked him slightly, knocking him down to Rufus's back again.

"This isn't up for debate," Jin said, and took a deep breath, then let it out. Suddenly Lena was on Rufus's back, and Jin was kneeling in her place, his arms bulging with muscles. "Consider your wish fulfilled, Thomas!" he shouted at the Last Knight. "Because this might be the last one I'm able to grant!"

"You'll *never* be free, djinn," the dragon laughed. "Stay behind, and I'll ensure you will be lost in shadow for all eternity."

Jin locked eyes with Lena, and he slowly smiled, sending one last burst of light through the green sphere. "Eh, it'll still be worth it."

"No!" Lena shouted, but she was already too late. Jin

sprouted a third arm and picked Rufus up. He leaned back to throw them . . .

Only for the dragon, Lena's mother, and the Last Knight to all scream in pain. One by one, the three horrors exploded in a burst of light so bright it blinded them all.

"What happened?" Lena shouted.

"Was it the power of my sacrifice?" Jin asked excitedly. "Did I just destroy them with how awesome I am?"

And then someone laughed, low and guttural.

"Not exactly, little boy," a new voice growled.

"That was us," said a second voice, this one even more gravelly.

"The scariest thing in these woods," snarled a third voice. "And look what we just caught! Seems like we'll be eating well tonight, eh, Sisters?"

CHAPTER 20

ell, *that* didn't sound good. Jin quickly erased and re-formed his eyes, so that he'd no longer be blinded as badly, then squinted into the still-bright light.

There were definitely three of them, though they didn't look particularly large. Not that their size mattered, considering they'd just taken down three shadow creatures without any effort.

Rufus began to hiss, backing away from the newcomers as his hair stood up on end. Also probably not a great sign.

"We're not afraid of you," Lena said, stepping forward with her arm up to shade her eyes. "Turn down your light and face us. There's no way we're letting you *eat* us!"

The three laughed again, which didn't seem like a particularly positive response. "Eat you?" one said.

"Why would we do that?" asked another.

The light dimmed around them, revealing three girls, each about Lena's height and age from what Jin could tell using his magical senses. Each one had hair almost to the ground, braided into matching cords down their backs, with huge fur cloaks that completely covered their bodies, all but for their hands. And all three girls held a spear with a glowing blade at the end.

Other than the color of their fur cloaks, the girls could have been triplets, they looked so identical. But one dressed in black fur, one in brown, and the third in gray, matching each of their hair colors.

And all were so beautiful it almost hurt to look at them.

"Who *are* you?" Jin asked, though somehow he felt like he already knew.

At his side, Jill sighed. "Oh great. *The wolf sisters*. Just what we needed, the three daughters of the big bad Wolf King."

Right, the Wolf King. Jin had gotten that far in the *Half Upon a Time* Story Book. An enormous wolf, larger than Rufus, the Wolf King could also turn human, which explained how he had three very human-looking daughters.

But that also meant they could probably turn into some pretty intimidating wolves themselves.

"We're hunters," the black-fur-cloaked girl said, answering Jin's question with an evil grin. "And maybe the girl has a point. They *do* look like they'd make for a good meal."

"Stop it, Tala," the gray-fur-cloaked girl said, rolling her eyes. "We *are* hunters, but not for food. That's not the job. We're only out here to find humans lost in the shadow and bring them into the city for judgment."

"Or for *dinner*," said the black-fur girl, Tala, then laughed.

The brown-fur girl just growled at Jin and his friends, low and menacingly.

"I'm Coni," the gray-fur girl said. "This is Tala, and Susi." She nodded at Black Fur and Brown Fur in order. "Now, let's get moving. The shadow seemed to really want you three, and we won't get paid if it steals you away from us."

She was both right and wrong about the shadow wanting the three of them. It did desire *one* of them, and Jin unfortunately knew who it was now.

While the dragon, Malevolent, had blustered about imprisoning him out loud, inwardly the shadow had been . . . communicating with Jin in his mind, just as he'd done with Jill earlier. The shadow had offered power, the power to raze the world and rule whatever was left.

EMBRACE YOUR BIRTHRIGHT, DJINN, the shadow dragon had thought to him. *THESE LESSER CREATURES YOU SURROUND YOURSELF WITH DEMEAN YOU. THEY WOULD DESTROY YOU, AS THEY'VE HUNTED AND IMPRISONED DJINN THROUGHOUT TIME.*

Oddly, this wasn't the first time he'd felt something like this. The last time had been when he'd first held the Spark, back in the Golden King's castle.

Both the shadow and the Spark spoke with the *same voice*. And that raised all kinds of interesting questions.

"Excuse me," Shefin said, crossing his arms indignantly as he disrupted Jin's train of thought. "But we won't be going anywhere with you until we know what you intend for us." Jin considered flicking him off into the woods and leaving him there but held himself back in case Lena would be mad.

Tala's eyes widened as she noticed the Lilliputian boy. "*Four* of you?" she said. "And look how adorable you are!" She stalked forward, her eyes bright with excitement, and slunk down to Shefin's height as she neared. "I think I'm going to keep you as a pet. Would you like that, little guy?"

Despite his best efforts, a laugh escaped Jin's lips, and Shefin turned to glare at him. "What?" Jin asked. "You *are* adorable."

"I am a *prince*!" Shefin shouted. "And future emperor of Lilliput!"

Tala stiffened like she'd just been struck and bared her teeth at the boy. "A Lilliputian?" she growled. "*This* is what you look like? We've fought your Faceless a thousand times, but I had no idea you were this small. Serves me right for not cracking open the armor to see what was inside."

Coni, the gray-furred girl, lowered her light-tipped spear and aimed it at Shefin. "The city council should pay us well for such an odd group."

Susi, the third girl, just growled in response and aimed her spear at Lena.

Anger crashed over Jin like a wave at the sight of Lena in danger, and he immediately swung his arm out, lengthening it as he did, and slammed it into the spear, knocking it slightly aside. Considering he'd intended to send it flying into the forest, that wasn't so great. Turned out the girl was stronger than he'd thought. *"Don't you threaten her,"* he said, trying to make his voice as low as the wolf girls' and failing dramatically.

"A shape-shifter?" Coni said, her spear now pointed at Jin. "You're all just full of surprises, aren't you? We really will eat well tonight."

"Assuming the council accepts these nonhumans," Tala said, frowning. "We're not supposed to bring in anyone exposed to shadow magic."

Lena stiffened at Tala's words and moved to stand in front of the group. "I didn't want to have to do this," she said, cracking her knuckles as she looked at the wolf girls dangerously, "but I'm not going to let you hurt anyone. These are my friends. And this one is my guide." She nodded at Shefin, who snorted. "I don't want to fight you, but I will."

In spite of her words, Jin could sense an excitement in Lena and wondered who she was trying to fool, the wolf girls or herself.

"Tell her not to bother," Jill said. "None of you can beat them. Not even Lena. They're *good*. Their father taught them well."

Susi aimed her spear at them again, while the other two smiled brightly, looking just as excited as Lena seemed to feel. "I hope you're not just some human," Tala said, grinning enough to show some sharp fangs. "That would be *so* disappointing."

"She's not," Coni said, narrowing her eyes and smiling even wider. "There's something different about her. Something . . . *fun*."

"Me first," Susi growled, the first words Jin had heard come out of her mouth. "I call it!"

"Jin, you have to stop her," Jill said, moving to stand in front of him. Oddly, she almost looked worried. "They're too *powerful*. Their mother is a literal dream woman, and their father is one of the most powerful warriors who ever lived. They're going to hurt Lena if she fights them!"

That familiar feeling of rage bubbled back up in Jin's chest at Jill's words, and he teleported to stand between Lena and the wolf girls. "This is *not* happening," he said, growing to twice his usual size and giving himself all the muscles he could think of. "We will defend ourselves if we have to, but would prefer to be taken to this city of yours, as you said."

"We're not taking you there for your enjoyment," Tala said. "The city council pays us to find anyone lost in the shadow, and then judges whether they're allowed to stay, or if they'll be thrown back into the shadow. They should find your little group *very* interesting."

"Which means we can finally afford to eat," Coni said, her eyes still bright over the prospect of a fight. "You're the first people we've found out here in *ages*."

"Then bring us in!" Jin said, spreading his arms wide. "You'll all eat, we'll meet this council of yours, and everyone goes home happy." Assuming they got judged correctly, that was, but how hard could *that* be? Jin and Lena were amazing! And maybe they could just pretend not to know Shefin.

The wolf sisters seemed to consider this, turning to each other and growling in low voices. Behind him, Jin could feel Lena's disappointment, but he could sense some relief there as well. Something was going on with her, but whatever it was could wait until this immediate danger was over.

"Okay," Coni said, as Tala and Susi looked slightly disappointed about the lack of a fight. "We'll bring you in. But one wrong move, and we'll see how tough you all are."

"Fair," Jin said, and shrank back to his usual size. "We'll be good, I promise."

"That was almost diplomatic!" Jill said, staring at him with wide eyes. "What happened to you? Did the fairy queens change your personality completely?"

No, he told her in her mind. *They just released my inhibitions. And in doing so, they unlocked my knowledge.*

Then he gasped out loud. Wait, *what?*

CHAPTER 21

As the three girls in fur escorted them through the remaining shadow toward the light of the city, Lena tried to keep herself between her friends and the newcomers, but the girls seemed to realize what she was doing and shifted into a triangle formation, surrounding them.

"Stop worrying so much," said the gray-haired girl, Coni. "I told you: we're going to bring you to the council. Until then, you're safe with us."

It didn't seem like they had much of a choice. But at least the spears the girls carried did seem to keep the shadows away, if only out of range of the light. Farther in the darkened woods, the shadow tentacles seethed like an angry ocean, continually pushing toward the edge of the light, only to pull back as the light struck them.

"Who *are* you three?" Lena asked Coni. "It must take someone pretty strong to go out in the shadow like you do."

"Seems like I could ask you the same thing," Coni said, shrugging. The city was growing closer now, and Lena could start making out its walls covered in torches glowing a brilliant blue through the darkness. Did those torches act somehow like their Lilliputian ring? Apparently so, as the shadow didn't seem to be approaching the walls at all.

Or maybe there was something *worse* than the darkness inside the city. The idea that there might be some sort of Trial of Wrath awaiting Lena made her almost wish they could just pass it by, keep on moving toward Lilliput. But without the sisters' light spears, there was no way they'd make it through the shadow. "What's some human girl doing with a shape-shifter, a giant cat, and a Lilliputian in the middle of the shadowlands?"

"I'm no human," she said, still distracted thinking about the potential trial. "I'm a giant, actually. So keep that in mind if you decide to fight."

Coni laughed, the sound both grating and melodic somehow. "Aren't you a bit short for a giant?"

"Who's a giant?" asked Tala, the black-haired girl.

"All of you," Shefin said bitterly, which made Tala laugh as well.

"I'm *not* short," Lena said through clenched teeth. "I'm exactly the size I'm supposed to be. And I don't care if you believe me or not. I'm just warning you."

Coni looked at her for a moment, then launched out with her spear, driving it right at Lena's side. Lena leapt backward instinctually and grabbed the spear right behind the blade, yanking it out of the girl's hands . . .

Only for Jin to teleport right next to her, ready for a fight. "Whoa!" Lena shouted at the girl, trying to keep the wolf and the genie apart. "What are you doing?"

"What did I tell you?" Jin shouted at Coni, growing himself back to his fighting form. "Do *not* touch her!"

"Aw, don't worry so much shape-shifter," Coni said, her eyes wide with both surprise and excitement. "I just wanted to see if she was really a giant." She turned back to Lena. "And I might even believe it now. You're *strong*!"

"Or you're getting weaker, sister," Tala said, but she seemed to be giving Lena an appraising look.

"How strong is she?" Susi asked, and Lena turned to find the third sister eying her dangerously, which didn't exactly help. "Stronger than Father?"

"Much stronger," Coni said, nodding. "You should have

fought us, giant! That would have been a *great* battle."

"It's not too late yet . . . ," Susi said, slowly raising her spear.

"I'm not fighting you," Lena told them, wishing she'd just dodged the spear and let it go. She put a hand on Jin's arm, and he slowly returned to his normal size, though he didn't look happy about it. "I'm trying . . . *not* to fight so much."

The three sisters just looked at one another in confusion. "Why?" Tala asked.

"That's so *wrong*," Susi said.

"Seriously," Coni agreed. "You're *made* to fight. Why wouldn't you want to? Don't you enjoy humiliating your enemies?"

"Driving them screaming before you?" Tala asked, her eyes alight with excitement.

Susi threw her head back and howled, a sound that made even Jin shudder in fear.

Lena just stared at them, now just as confused as they'd been a moment ago. "But I thought wanting to fight makes you vulnerable to the shadow magic. Aren't you worried you'll get taken over by it?"

The three sisters shared another look, then burst out laughing. "No?" Coni said, as if it made no sense to her at all. "Why would we be worried?"

"It's a lot easier to be brave when you've got light spears, I suppose," Shefin pointed out.

Susi grinned at him, then tossed the spear to the ground and walked out of the light created by the Lilliputian sphere and her sisters' weapons. She turned to face the shadow in the darkness and howled again, almost taunting it.

The shadow reacted immediately, rushing for her with several different tendrils, but she immediately dodged beneath the first, then leapt out of the way as more attacked. The shadow hissed in annoyance, but retreated as Susi's sisters approached with their spears.

"It's all about facing your fear," Susi said, standing back up and returning to the light as her sisters pushed them to continue on once more. "Though it helps to not actually be afraid of anything."

Shefin's mouth had dropped at the display, but he found his voice again at her words. "Oh stop it," he said. "*Everyone's* afraid of something."

"Nah," Tala said.

"It's such a waste of time, being afraid," Coni pointed out. "And in here, it gets you taken by the shadow, so it's smarter to just . . . not be."

"You should try it next time," Tala pointed out.

"That's not how fear works!" Shefin shouted. "You don't get to just decide not to be afraid; you just *are*."

"Sounds like *you* just are," Coni said, and Shefin growled at her. She laughed and growled back, making the Lilliputian back up a few steps on Rufus's back. "Talk to your giant. She's not afraid, are you, giant?"

Lena couldn't believe any of this. "Of course I am. Shefin is right, you can't just decide not to be." She paused. "My kind is . . . we're made from the shadow. Because of that, we're vulnerable to it. If it took me over . . ."

Coni gave her an odd look. "The shadow made you? So what? It probably made my family too. And the goblins, and the ogres, and all kinds of fun stuff."

"Is it controlling you now?" Tala asked, narrowing her eyes.

"No, of course not," Lena said.

"Then who cares what made you strong?" Coni said. "Our father did some pretty terrible things. Does that mean we will too?"

"Maybe, but only because we *want* to," Tala said, grinning dangerously.

Coni rolled her eyes. "It doesn't matter who or what made you, giant. All that matters is who you are. Who you *decide* to be."

Lena blinked, not sure what to even say to that. Unfortunately, she didn't have any more time to consider the girls' words, as they'd arrived at the city wall, the blue glow from the torches pushing any further shadow away.

Above them on the wall, someone was staring down with disgust.

"Any shadow infections, wolves?" the guard shouted.

"Come down and we'll show you," Coni replied, and the guard glared at her. "Open the gate, human. The council will want to judge our prey."

"Dirty animals," the guard muttered, and disappeared behind the wall. A moment later, a large metal gate began creaking open, but Lena couldn't believe what he'd just said.

"He was so cruel!" she said, almost in wonder. "Doesn't that bother you?"

Tala snorted. "That the *humans* don't like us? It might, if any of them were worth something. But don't expect to find any diamonds in the rough here. Not in the town of Charm."

A moment passed as the gate continued to open, and then Lena jumped as Jin shouted out of nowhere, "Okay, I get it— it's your city! *Stop yelling at me!*"

CHAPTER 22

"You don't understand!" Jill shouted at Jin, pointing up at the walls above them. "This is the city that my uncle, even my brother, once ruled over, from a castle . . ." She looked around, then shook her head. "Well, I don't know where the castle is. Somewhere in the shadow. But this is like my *home*, Jin! How did I not know this was where we were going?"

Jin started to respond, then switched back to his mental communication, not wanting to reveal anything else to the wolf girls. He was already annoyed enough at both Jill and himself for shouting what he just had out loud. *Probably because it wasn't in the shadowlands before, as far as you knew. Your body's been a statue in the Golden King's palace for a while, and the king's been spreading the darkness over these kingdoms since he took over.*

You wouldn't have even considered that Charm might have ended up covered in shadow.

She glared at him. "We really need to talk about all this knowledge you suddenly have. You said the fairy queens unlocked it? What does *that* mean?"

The others had started moving through the gate, though, so Jin just shook his head. *It's always been there, but I couldn't access it myself. But we'll talk about it later. Come on, before we get left behind.*

"Yeah, great, because getting led around by the daughters of the Wolf King is such a brilliant idea," Jill said as they followed Lena and the rest inside the city. "You read all about him. How do *you* feel about listening to the girls he raised?"

Jin shrugged. *I don't trust them, but not because of their parents. They've obviously left home, so it's not like the Wolf King is controlling them or something. And if they are on their own, who cares who their father is?*

"You're changing," Jill said, still irritated. "This new you, the one who knows things and is all mature? I don't like it."

He stuck out his tongue at her. *Yeah, well, I don't like you, either!*

She laughed. "There's the genie I know. Now come on, you're getting left behind."

He sent her a few choice words, then hurried to catch up.

Now that they were in the city, the wolf sisters closed ranks around the rest of them, though oddly it felt less intimidating and more protective. The residents of Charm weren't exactly living up to the city's name, as the nicest ones merely slammed their shutters closed or turned and walked away at the sight of them. The less-nice ones offered up their opinions on who Lena and her friends must be, and how exactly they were destroying the city.

"You're *all* cursed by the shadow!" one man shouted, then threw a rock, which Coni easily knocked to the ground with her spear, otherwise ignoring the man. "Get out of our city, and stop polluting it with your foul magic!"

"Animals!" a woman shouted, her face red with anger as the wolves led them farther into the city. "You belong in the dark like the rest of your kind."

Wonderful city you've got here, Jin pointed out to Jill, who seemed just as surprised as he was.

"I don't know what's going on!" she said, wide-eyed at the various insults being thrown their way. "They were *never* like that to us!"

That's because you look like them. So do Lena and I, for that matter. But Rufus and Shefin stand out, and they definitely *hate the wolf sisters. I'm surprised they've stuck around here.*

"Me too, honestly," Jill said, just as another man began screaming at Susi. The brown-haired girl paused, turned to him, then let out a growl from deep in her belly, and the man yelped, then took off running.

"Oh, Susi, you shouldn't even respond," Coni said, but she was grinning.

"You're right. I should just *silently* eat them," Susi said, turning on a woman who was glaring at the wolf sisters. "Maybe I will, if one of them says another word."

The woman blinked, then turned and ran, joining various other townspeople who all used the opportunity to make themselves scarce. And just moments after entering the city, Jin and his friends were alone on the streets of Charm.

"Maybe . . . we should try to understand the city's people?" Lena said quietly. "They're afraid, and using their anger to cover it."

"Oh, I understand them," Coni said, her eyes narrowing dangerously. "Everything you just said was true, and that's why I want to throw them all out into the shadow. *You* all were afraid of us too—"

"*I* wasn't," Jin and Shefin said at the same time, then glared at each other.

"But you didn't call us *animals*," Coni finished. "Sorry, but I'm not feeling any kind of compassion for the city dwellers. They're certainly not showing us any."

Lena slowly nodded but still looked conflicted. This was about the trials she'd mentioned earlier, Jin decided, but even his newfound knowledge didn't give him any insights into how to help her with whatever they might be. So instead, he bumped gently into her, just like Rufus did when he wanted to be petted, then walked alongside her quietly, hoping she would sense his support.

Even Jill didn't say much from that point, though she kept making small noises of recognition as they continued, pointing at a house here or an inn there. At one point, she gasped slightly, and Jin turned to find her staring at a large manor, now boarded up and abandoned.

What is it? he asked. *Don't tell me it's haunted. We're full up on invisible people.*

"Clearly you didn't get a sense of humor along with all that knowledge," Jill said, barely paying him any attention. "This is . . . this *was* May's house. My sister-in-law May. A long time ago, but still. It's where her father lived, and her stepmother and stepsisters." She shuddered. "You can practically feel the evil, can't you? Maybe it *is* haunted."

Jin squinted at the house, trying to take in as much information as he could. Somehow he already knew most of it, that May had been meant to grow up here, under the abuse of her stepmother and stepsisters, and that Merriweather of all people had helped May free herself, apparently by providing a dress and a pumpkin carriage to go to a ball.

That was . . . unexpected. Though it did track with what Jill had said about the fairy queens, that they liked their romance.

Oddly, Jin also recognized that something was missing. *Didn't there use to be goblins here, in this city?* he thought to Jill. *Back when the Wicked Queen controlled it?*

"Yeah, but considering how welcoming the people are now, I'm not surprised they all left," Jill said. "It's kind of awful. We spent a lot of time making sure the goblins were treated equally after everything, since May was sort of their new leader. They hadn't been in control of their actions any more than—"

Than the Last Knight?

Jill rolled her eyes. "Maybe. I don't know. I just can't trust him. You were there; you heard the things he said to Shefin. There's something about this plan of his that I don't understand yet, but I will. Why take the risk on using shadow magic himself? He must have a really good reason, and it's *not* just to beat the Golden King."

That much felt right. Why *would* the Last Knight take such a chance? Thomas had mentioned someone controlling things—

Jill sighed, interrupting Jin's line of thinking as she moved away from May's old house. "We're falling behind again. You really need to stop getting distracted."

Right, Jin said, rolling his eyes. There'd be time to figure out the mystery of the Last Knight later, anyway. For now, they needed to concentrate on just stopping the Golden King and locking away the shadow.

That, and keep Lena safe through it all. Whether she had feelings for Jin or not.

Ugh, *what* had he just thought? Was this some kind of terrible selflessness that came with the knowledge? Gross. What kind of horrible curse *was* this knowledge?

"You know, I guess we should be thankful that May's stepmother isn't around, at least," Jill said as they caught up to the others and began climbing some marble steps toward a large marble building with columns in the center of town, most likely the location of the city council. "You can't imagine how bad she was, or May's stepsisters. There's shadow magic evil, and then there's *them*."

She had a point. Not that Jin had read the Story Books that far, but he still knew how May's stepmother and stepsisters had screamed at May to serve them throughout the day, forcing her to do all the chores while bemoaning their lives.

All in all, Jin was fairly glad they weren't around too.

"Ah, my wolf servants, back from the outside world with a new delivery," said a voice inside the keep. Two guards emerged first, then separated, revealing three women.

"Oh *no*," Jill said, her eyes widening. "*No, no, no!* It's *her*!"

"Councilors," Coni said, greeting the three newcomers. "Per our agreement, we've brought you new shadowland travelers to be judged. Special ones, this time."

A regal woman in an elaborate gown made of gold stepped forward, glaring down at Jin, Lena, Rufus, and Shefin. She was flanked by two younger women, both looking disgusted, and though Jin hadn't seen pictures of them in the Story Book, he instantly knew their identities.

"Yes, I suppose you have," May's evil stepmother said. "Now what kind of *filth* have you found this time, Wolf Princess?"

CHAPTER 23

Susi growled softly at Lena's side, and Lena couldn't blame her. Who *was* this horrible woman, the councilor? Even Coni seemed ready to take a bite out of her, but somehow managed to hold herself back.

"We found these four in the woods, facing off against the shadow," the gray-haired girl said. "As you can see, one of them appears to be a Lilliputian—"

The older councilor sniffed, while the younger two wrinkled their noses. "Midas can't even keep his own servants in line anymore," the older woman said. "It's a wonder he hasn't lost everything to those horrible rebels." She glanced over Jin, then turned to Lena, smiling slightly. "And what about you humans? How did you end up traveling with a smelly, oversized cat and one of the Faceless?"

Lena gritted her teeth so hard her jaw hurt. "They're my friends, actually," she said. "Well, not Shefin. Rufus, though, my very *not* smelly cat, is my *best* friend."

"Ouch," Jin mumbled as the three councilors looked even more disgusted.

"You made this creature of shadow your *pet*?" one of the younger ones said.

"It reminds me of that monkey that May had, remember that?" the other younger one said. *"Horrifying."*

Creature of shadow? *Rufus?* Lena's face turned red with anger as she took a step closer to the councilors, pushing down so hard that the marble stairs trembled beneath her feet. The three councilors' disgusted looks turned to surprise. "Well, he's better than any *human* I know," Lena told them, her palms hurting from digging her nails into them.

"I knew there was a reason I liked you," Coni whispered. "But if you want to be allowed to stay here, you should show some respect. They're not exactly full of mercy for those lost in the shadow."

Her words made Lena freeze. Was this the Trial of Wrath? If so, she had already been nearly overtaken by rage. She couldn't let these women upset her any further, not if she was going to stay calm and pass the trial!

"What *are* you?" the older woman demanded of Lena, backing away now. "You're of the shadow yourself, aren't you? *Aren't you?*"

"We told you, no creatures of shadow are to be brought into the city!" one of the younger ones said, pointing at Coni. "You might have infected us all with their darkness!"

Susi growled again, and Tala sighed. "I'm beginning to think we're not getting paid tonight," she said to her sisters.

"We lived up to our contract, Councilors," Coni said, not looking any more thrilled than her sisters. "You said you'd pay us if we brought travelers to Charm, where they could be judged. We've done just that. *None* of them are shadow infected."

"We meant *human* travelers, not these . . . *creatures*," one of the younger woman spat. "Why would you ever think we wanted their kind here? We forced all of the goblins out years ago. If we didn't tolerate *those* monsters, we certainly won't accept these unnatural things!"

Lena had fought Faceless, shadows, and even the Golden King, but never had she wanted to punch someone as much as she did the three councilors. But just like she'd said about the townspeople of Charm, these women must have been through something horrible to act like this toward others. If she concentrated on trying to understand them, to empathize even, she could hold back the anger and not do anything rash.

Honestly, if this *was* the trial, it was much harder than Lena had expected. Because while knocking out the leaders of a city wouldn't exactly be proving herself worthy, it'd definitely feel *so good*.

But she wasn't about to fail without a fight. Or, well, not fighting, as the case may be.

"My lady, maybe we got off on the wrong foot," Lena said, spreading her arms out wide as she bowed. "You are right to be afraid of the shadow, and we can't fault you for that. But whatever we are, we're not under its control."

"You think I care?" the older woman shouted, waving her fingers at them like she was shooing away an insect. "Get these monsters out of our city, *now*. Or consider our contract void."

"I knew it was a bad idea to pay these brainless wolves to keep the undesirables out," one of the younger women said.

"Of course they'd look for their own kind instead," said the other younger woman.

This time, Tala and Susi stepped forward, only for Coni to growl at them and pull them back. "We seem to have made a mistake," the gray-haired girl said, lowering her head. "We'll escort these four to the outer gate and send them on their way."

Lena felt her understanding for the three women evaporate, and part of her wasn't upset about it. It was one thing to have experienced pain and suffering in your past, but to throw her and her friends back out into the shadow? Even a completely innocent creature like Rufus? That wasn't okay, no matter how much understanding a person had.

"Please, we mean no harm," Lena said, desperately trying to stay calm in spite of how much she wanted to toss all three women into the air and juggle them until they threw up. "This was our fault, coming into your city without getting permission first. What can we do to make things right?"

"You can *get out*," the older councilor said. "Take your foul self and your vile traveling companions as far away as you can. I don't want you finding your way back here ever again." She shuddered. "The city of Charm has become an oasis for humanity, hidden away in the Golden King's darkness. None of you belong here, not among your betters. You make me *sick*, all of you! Now go back to the shadow where you belong!"

Lean stiffened like she'd been hit, and a roaring filled her ears. "Enough," she whispered, looking down at the ground.

"It's *never* enough for your kind," one of the younger women said. "All you do is take from the good human beings, never give. So maybe *we* have had enough!"

Never . . . give? Lena took a step forward, her whole body trembling. All thoughts of the trial, the fairy queens, and her mission disappeared, replaced by too many ideas of what she could do to these . . . *monsters*. And that's what they were, she knew, the same thing the councilors were calling Lena and her friends. "What are you doing?" the older councilor said as Lena took another step closer, barely able to think. "Get back. Guards, stop her!"

The human guards moved in, but the wolf sisters blocked them, holding them back with their spears. "Sorry," Coni said with a grin. "This is just getting interesting. Let's see where it goes, shall we?"

Susi and Tala both smiled as well.

"Get away from me!" the older councilor shouted at Lena, backing away now as the two younger women hid behind her, using her like a shield.

"You think we're evil?" Lena said, her voice low and icy cold. "I could prove you right, you know. It would be so *easy*."

"Don't hurt me!" one of the younger councilors begged. "I

never thought you were bad—it was them!" She pointed at the other two, who also quickly began claiming innocence and blaming each other.

"What are you going to do, giant girl?" Coni whispered, so low only Lena could hear her. "They deserve it, whatever you decide. The whole city does."

Lena nodded, the roaring in her ears getting louder. She took another step forward, and now the older councilor fell, tripping against the other two, and the three all went down into a heap, wailing and pleading.

"You're not a monster!" one shouted at Lena. "Please, we don't deserve this!"

"That's where you're wrong," Coni growled. "You've broken your contract with us, tried to cheat us. That's all over now."

And then, right before Lena's eyes, the girl transformed into a wolf the size of Rufus.

The three councilors began screaming all at once. More guards appeared, but Susi and Tala leapt forward, changing into wolves in mid-jump, and knocked the guards aside. Coni, meanwhile, padded forward, growling quietly.

"I've never actually eaten someone before," she said.

"Unfortunately for you, it's been a long time since you paid us, so we're *awfully* hungry."

"No," Lena said, stepping in front of the wolf. "These three are *mine*."

Coni looked up at her with wolfen eyes. "I wasn't actually going to eat them," she growled low. "Just scare them."

"They don't need to be scared," Lena said, her eyes narrowing. "They need to *learn*."

And with that, she reached down and picked the older councilor up by her robe, dangling her off the ground.

"Please! I'll do anything!" the woman shouted, trembling with fright. "Don't hurt me!"

Lena looked up into her eyes, her rage making her heart beat so loud she could hear it in her ears.

And then she set the woman down on her feet and moved to help the other two up as well.

"What is this?" Coni growled, and her sisters mumbled something equally as disappointed. "I thought you were going to teach them a lesson."

Lena took in a deep, shuddering breath, not sure she could answer. But no matter how angry she felt, no matter how much these women might deserve to feel all the pain they'd caused others, that wasn't going to change anything.

"Take what they owe you," Lena said to Coni. "All of it. You had a deal."

The three councilors looked stunned at this. "Wait, but that's *ours*—" one said, then went quiet as Susi growled at her.

"No, it's not," Lena said, forcing her fists to unclench and wiping her sweaty hands on her tunic. "You had a deal. And the wolf sisters did as they were asked."

Coni just stared at Lena for a moment, then sighed, which was an odd sound for a wolf to make. "Take all the food they owe us, Sisters," she ordered, still looking Lena in the eye. "Or anything else of value to make up their debt. If you have to, leave them to the mercy of their fellow humans. But . . . don't hurt them."

"Awww!" both her sisters said at once.

"Do it!" Coni growled, and the other two wolves padded into the marble building, pushing past the three councilors so closely that the women all flinched.

Lena took another breath, just trying to calm herself down.

"I would really have enjoyed biting them," Coni said, turning back to her human form. "You owe me one for that, giant girl. Couldn't you have at least roughed them up a bit?"

Lena gave her a confused look. "Oh, I'd never do that. With my strength, I might seriously have hurt them." She shrugged. "Taking their things seemed like it'd be more upsetting for them anyway."

Coni laughed, which helped Lena's mood just a bit. "You're not wrong there."

"You would leave us desolate?" one of the younger councilors asked. "Please, have mercy!"

"This *is* mercy," Coni growled, but Lena shook her head.

"You owed them," she said simply to the councilors. "And you refused to pay. Now, maybe next time, you'll keep your word."

The other young councilor started to respond, but a look from Coni made her go silent instead.

As Lena's fury lessened, shame took its place: she knew she'd let her rage overwhelm her, exactly as the fairy queens had warned her. If this was the Trial of Wrath, she'd definitely failed it, acting out of anger instead of peace or understanding. And just because the councilors weren't hurt didn't mean anything, not if the trial was about overcoming her rage.

Yes, even apart from their vile beliefs, the women *had* cheated Coni and her sisters. And Lena firmly believed the wolf sisters were owed what they were taking. But even if she'd done the right thing for the wolves, the *fair* thing, it hadn't been for calm, rational reasons.

No, it was because the horrible women had enraged her.

Which meant she'd proven exactly the wrong thing to the Illumination of Worthiness. Had Lena just doomed the entire world because she couldn't get beyond her anger at these women? The thought pushed the remaining indignation out of her mind, leaving behind only dread and sorrow.

There were still two more challenges, though. Maybe it wasn't too late? Maybe she could still prove herself worthy, prove that she *could* overcome the shadow within herself?

Because if she couldn't, the whole world would suffer, and it'd be all her fault.

CHAPTER 24

A human-looking Coni led her sisters in wolf form out of town with Jin and his friends on Rufus at their side. The wolves had multiple belts of pouches draped over their backs filled with food and whatever treasures the councilors had stashed away, which made Jin curious, but now was probably not the time to see what they'd found.

As the gates shut behind them, the guards began yelling down insults but immediately went quiet as Coni aimed her spear at them, ready to throw.

"Goodbye, Charm," Jill said sadly. "You're somehow worse now than when the Wicked Queen controlled you. Just a fine showing, all around."

Jin didn't have anything to add to that as the sisters led them back into the woods, and immediately the shadow closed in around them. Fortunately, Coni carried all three of the wolves' spears now, and the shadow writhed angrily but couldn't pass through their light.

Jin glanced at the thrashing darkness, feeling its anger even now. Just as the Spark had, the shadow wanted his power, his magic. And he wasn't too proud of the fact that there was something tempting about its offer, to rid the world of humans and anything else that might get in his way. While some of the Cursed City's residents were certainly friends of his, Jin hadn't exactly been impressed with the rest of the species so far. Between the Golden King and the city of Charm, he was halfway ready to say goodbye to the entire lot of them.

"We should never have wasted our time here," Coni said as the city disappeared in the darkness, not even a light getting through now. "I'm not really sure where to go next, though."

"We haven't finished our trial," Susi growled, and Lena jumped. She seemed extremely on edge after the visit to Charm, which Jin couldn't fault her for. Not exactly his favorite place either. "We can't leave the shadowlands yet."

"It's not actually an official trial," Tala said with a gravelly laugh. "Father just wanted us to learn to get along. He must not have known you're basically feral."

Susi snarled, then snapped at her sister, who snapped back. Coni immediately moved between them and smacked both their snouts. "Are you serious with this? We've got outsiders around. No infighting in front of others, Sisters."

"Yes, Coni," her sisters said in unison.

Not sure what to make of any of *that*, Jin decided to make a peace offering. This whole diplomacy thing had worked so far, so it couldn't hurt to try again. "There *are* other settlements in the shadow, if you want to stay here for some odd reason," he said, and the three sisters all turned to look at him. "The closest one is just a few days away."

"Except we're in a hurry," Lena said, sounding both exhausted and panicked at the same time. Probably due to whatever trials she'd been talking about earlier, which he'd have to find out more about soon if he was going to be any help to her. "Rufus can get us there quickly, though, so maybe you can just tell them where it is, Jin?"

The sisters all began to laugh. "You think this cat can move faster than us?" Coni asked. "I can outrun him in *human* form, let alone as a wolf!"

"Rufus is the fastest there is!" Rufus interjected, which was a good sign. The cat had been staying mostly quiet in the shadow, and Jin couldn't blame him, given how terrible it was here. But him standing up to the wolves suggested that he was feeling at least a little more comfortable now. Probably helped that the wolves' magical spear lights were quite a bit more steady than the Lilliputian ring had been.

"I've met faster turtles than you, cat," Tala said to Rufus with a snort, and Susi just growled playfully at him. Rufus didn't appear to notice the playful part and hissed back in turn.

Meanwhile, Lena seemed to be getting either annoyed or nervous about all of this, so Jin decided to step in. "He's wearing Seven League Boots," he said to the wolf sisters. "They can jump the wearer that far with every step."

"Seven *leagues*?" Coni said, raising an eyebrow. "Not bad, feline. But I'm guessing he can't do that in the shadow, can he?"

"I wouldn't recommend it," Jill said, and Jin passed her words along.

"We haven't tried it," Shefin said to Coni. "But I wouldn't bet on our protective spell lasting much longer, even if the beast jumps with his boots."

"Well, that's not Rufus's fault!" Lena shouted, hugging her now-purring cat around the neck. "He's doing his best. The shadow is just too dangerous."

"Not for us," Coni said with a grin. Even her human teeth were impressively intimidating. "I'd say we could carry you all on our backs, but I think Rufus might be a bit large, even for me."

"Well, we can shrink him," Jin pointed out, then yelped as Lena stamped on his foot. "What was *that* for?"

"Can I talk to you for a moment?" she whispered, and yanked him backward before he could respond. The light from the sisters' spears didn't extend too far into the shadow, so Lena moved him to the absolute edge of it, with Shefin back on her shoulder. "We don't have *time* to help them right now," she whispered. "The shadow is going to reach the Cursed City soon, not to mention my parents' home in the clouds and the rest of the world!"

Jin nodded. "That's true, but we won't get far if we can't get through the shadow ourselves. I know *I* couldn't keep the happy thoughts coming, and I'm pretty amazing at everything. What if Shefin's right, and the Lilliputian ring fails? We'd be lost to the shadow."

The idea of the darkness infecting Lena physically hurt Jin, and there was no way he was going to allow that to happen. Shefin, sure, and maybe even her cat, but never Lena. But beyond that, the shadow seemed to really want Jin's power. And tempting or not, he wasn't ready to see what it might do with it.

And then there was the fact that the shadow and the Spark both sounded exactly the same in his head. At some point, their connection needed to be explored, but that would have to join the list of everything else he needed to consider more with his newfound knowledge.

"Maybe we're being too pessimistic," Shefin said. "Just because I haven't heard of any Lilliputians making it all the way through the shadowlands using the protective sphere doesn't mean it's impossible!"

Lena and Jin both turned to look at Shefin, then each other. "*That* would have been useful to know earlier," Lena said, shaking her head.

"I said I hadn't *heard* of any," Shefin pointed out. "That just means they probably made it across the shadow and are living quite well on the other side."

"*Anyway*, Jin has a point: we need the wolves' spears," Lena said. "I don't know what else to do, but I really do hate losing time for this."

"Coni was right that they can move faster through the woods than Rufus can," Jin pointed out. "So even if we waste some time getting them to the next town, we still might end up getting to Lilliput faster than on our own."

"Oh, just *go* with them already!" Jill said, sounding exasperated. "Is there anything you people *don't* discuss to death?"

"Hey! Ridiculous boys and girls!" Tala shouted. "Are we going or what?"

Lena glanced at Jin and then Shefin. "We are," she said finally, and strode back over to the wolves. "Rufus, I'm sorry about this, but I need you to wear your collar."

The cat didn't look thrilled but nodded. "If Lena says so. But Rufus is *still* faster than dogs." With that, he bent his head so that Lena could put the collar on. She pulled it out of her pouch and wrapped it around his neck, then fastened the clasp. As soon as the collar was closed, Rufus shrank down to normal cat size.

"Oh, that's fun!" Tala growled, staring down at Rufus hungrily. "Would make for an interesting hunt, wouldn't it?"

Lena picked Rufus up protectively, then grabbed Tala by her furry chin and stared deep into the wolf's eyes. *"You touch my boy,"* she hissed, her eyes narrowed and dangerous, *"I make you regret ever being born."*

Susi and Coni laughed, but Tala just whined as Lena didn't let go. Finally, the wolf nodded. "Okay, okay, he's off-limits. *Happy?"*

"You're my new favorite thing we've found in the woods, giant girl," Coni said, clapping Lena on the shoulder hard enough to make her stumble. "You act just like one of us!"

"It's *Lena*, not giant girl," she said, then pointed at the others. "And they're Jin, Shefin, and Rufus."

"Boring!" Susi growled.

"Yeah, really," Tala said, eyeing Lena warily. "Can we get a move on or what?"

"Where is this next oasis from the shadow, shape-shifter . . . I mean, Jin?" Coni asked.

"That way," Jin said pointing into the darkness. "And it's less an oasis, and more of a farm."

"A farm?" Jill said. "That sounds way too normal for how things are going. Is it a *dangerous* farm? Will they be farming *us*? What's the twist here?"

He looked at her, then at the wolves, wincing. *It* may *be a farm run by, um, animals,* he said in her mind.

Jill burst out laughing. "Oh, great suggestion, Jin! *That'll* go over well. I can't wait to see how adding three wolves into a farm run by, what, *pigs* or something, is going to go!"

CHAPTER 25

The wolves hadn't been wrong about their speed: As Coni loped along in wolf form below her, Lena could barely make out the shadows rushing past. She kept one hand tightly on Rufus, who had his own relatively tiny front paws on the wolf's shoulder, probably happy to not be the one carrying her for once. In her other hand, Lena held Coni's spear like a lance, its light separating the shadow before it, splitting it to either side, where it writhed helplessly.

Coni claimed each of the three spears' magic only worked for a third of a day, before needing twelve hours of rest. That helped explain why they'd gotten into a contract with Charm in the first place, since using all three spears at once would leave them vulnerable, so they needed a safe place to let the magic restore itself. Still, in an emergency, the sisters' three spears could cover the entire day by using them one at a time.

But with three wolves and four riders, just one spear wouldn't be enough. That meant they had at most eight hours before the spears' magic faded, leaving them with a ring that only worked on happy thoughts, and far too little happiness to fuel it with.

Part of her wondered about where the spears had come from. Susi had mentioned this was a trial of some kind, given by their father, it sounded like. But beyond that, the wolves hadn't been exactly forthcoming about their past.

But the wolf sisters' trial wasn't what currently filled Lena's thoughts, her heart racing for reasons other than the shadow. She knew she'd failed the Trial of Wrath; it wasn't even a question. But the fairy queens hadn't been clear about whether she needed to pass *all* the trials. Could she still convince the Illumination of Worthiness that she wasn't bad, just by passing the last two trials?

The answer had to be yes. Otherwise everyone was already doomed, and Lena couldn't, wouldn't accept that.

But that meant the last two trials, Warfare and Wickedness, were even more important than she'd feared. Wrath had seemed straightforward enough, and she'd still managed to fail. How hard would the next two be?

Just to the side of her neck, she heard Shefin sigh, holding tightly to the collar of her tunic. "I'm so useless," he whispered to himself, so quietly that Lena never would have heard it if he hadn't been sitting right next to her ear.

The pain in his voice distracted her from her own thoughts for a moment. "What do you mean?" she said, turning her head slightly so he could hear her voice over the wind. "You're our guide. You're not useless." Annoying, sure, and certainly not her true love—she couldn't imagine that of *anyone*—but not useless.

"You . . . weren't supposed to hear that," he said quietly. "But it's true, I am. The genie's doing the guiding now. All I did was point out the direction of the shadowlands, and then almost wet myself when the shadows attacked."

Lena paused, not sure what to say to that, and not particularly enjoying the thought that he'd been on her shoulder at the time. "We were *all* scared. And just because Jin knows where the protected spots are in the shadowlands doesn't mean we don't need you. Once we get to Lilliput, you're the one who can lead us inside the Golden King's castle. That's when you're really going to step up."

He snorted. "Oh, sure. The Last Knight will take one look

at me and send me back to his house again. He thinks I'm too small to be of any help to the revolution, Lena. What am I supposed to say to that?"

"'Don't judge people by their size?'" she said, raising an eyebrow. "Just a suggestion."

He laughed slightly. "Fair enough, except he's not wrong. I *am* a lot smaller than any of the other rebels. Yes, I'm younger than they are, but I'm even tiny for my age. You heard the shadow version of him. He was right: I have to be kept out of danger, or Lilliput would have one less heir to the emperor's throne."

Lena rolled her eyes. "You really need to stop bringing that up. No one cares if you're royalty."

Shefin choked slightly at that. "Oh, I see, you're trying to cheer me up? Brilliant job you're doing. *No one cares about you or your title, Shefin.*"

Wow, he really did make this harder than it needed to be. The magic mirror honestly couldn't have been more wrong, claiming he'd be her true love. "I'm saying that we can like you as a *person*, if you'd just let us. Stop acting so arrogant all the time. It doesn't matter if you're a royal or just a regular person, like the rest of us."

"Right, because you're such a regular person, with your super strength and genie friend." He sighed again. "What if I can't do this, Lena? What if we're in Lilliput, and the Last Knight tries to stop me from going to help you? Or worse, what if he lets me join you and I still mess it all up?"

"So basically, what if you've got the exact same worries I have?" She shrugged gently, making sure not to throw him off. "Sounds like we've got more in common than you thought."

"Unlike your common birth versus my royal one," he said.

"I'll tell you what," she said, once she was sure she had her irritation under control. "I'll make sure the Last Knight never even knows you're with us, so at least you'll have the chance to prove yourself. And in return, you just promise you'll do your best to help us stop the Golden King. Deal?"

"What kind of deal is *that*?" he asked. "I do all the hard work, and you agree to, what, hide me for a bit? Only a gullible sucker would accept any deal along those lines."

She blinked several times, half ready to flick him off her shoulder. Maybe *this* was the true Trial of Wrath, because it was starting to feel like just as much of a test as Charm had been. If she couldn't hold her temper with Shefin, though, then there was no way she'd be worthy.

"Fair . . . enough," she said through her gritted teeth. "You do whatever you want, as long as you get us in the Golden King's castle."

"Obviously I will," he said. "But I'm glad we had this talk, since it seems to have made you feel better."

"*Me* feel better?!" she shouted. "*That's* what you were doing?"

"Of course, and I'm glad it worked," he said, patting her shoulder. "Now shush, I have to come up with a plan. One does not simply *walk* into the Golden King's castle, after all."

Lena pushed her face into Rufus's head, just behind his hat, and let out a scream of frustration into his fur. He glanced back up at her questioningly, then blinked at her, one of the ways he showed his affection. "Lena is okay? Does the wind make her whiskers tingle too?"

"It would if I had them, little man," she said to him. "But we should be there soon—"

And just like that, Coni slowed to a walk, then stopped, sniffing the air.

"Do you smell that?" she said to her sisters as they slowed as well. "Magic, up ahead."

The two other wolves both lowered their heads and growled.

"Is it dangerous?" Lena asked, and Coni sniffed again.

"Can't tell," she growled. "Might be the farm, though."

"I'm sure it is," Jin said quickly. "Just a regular, everyday farm, certainly not strange in any way. But you know what would be fun? If we all make a promise not to eat anyone. Let's call it a contest, and see who can win. Who's with me?"

That was an odd thing to say, but Lena couldn't worry about it now. After all, a second protected oasis in the shadow meant the very likely possibility of the second trial, this one the Trial of Warfare.

And that meant no matter how regular, everyday this farm actually was, they were going to find danger inside.

The question was, would it be the farm itself . . . or Lena?

CHAPTER 26

A blue dome of light greeted them as the shadow parted, and Jin mentally prepared himself for what could end up being a wolf feeding frenzy. According to his knowledge—another thing he was going to have to spend more time thinking about, and why the fairy queen's release of his inhibitions had unlocked it—the animals here were intelligent and had grouped together for safety years ago.

"Let's all introduce ourselves in human form, just for the challenge," he said to the wolf sisters nervously. "That way we won't scare the farmers."

Susi, though, seemed distracted, sniffing loudly. "Do you smell that, Sisters?"

"I smell . . . something," Coni said. "Pigs? The scent is old, maybe months or more, but it's there."

Months old? But that didn't make any sense. Not that it seemed to bother the wolves, as Tala growled happily. "Pigs?" she said, drooling slightly. "That means fresh meat!"

Jin threw a panicked look at Lena, and she grasped the problem right away, jumping down from Coni's back with a small Rufus still in her arms. "Jin's right—we should all be in human form so we don't make them nervous," she said to the wolves. "And if the farmers let us in, we *can't* eat their livestock. They'd kick us out right away."

"Might be worth it," Tala said, and Susi grinned, showing far too many teeth.

"Enough," Coni told her sisters, then morphed into her human form. "Lena is right. We've used the spears too long without letting the magic recover, so right now, this farm is our only chance for rest. Let's not mess it up the moment we walk in, okay?"

"So, we can mess it up in an hour or so, then?" Tala asked, also changing to her human form. Coni shot her a death glare, but Tala just laughed.

"I hate my human form," Susi growled, but changed anyway, pouting. "And I *really* wanted a pig!"

Jin let out a sigh of relief and threw Lena a quick salute. She smiled slightly back, which sent a wave of joy through him. As much as he now knew Lena had no feelings for him, he still felt hope that she might develop them someday. . . .

Except . . . he knew better than that, somehow. Just like he'd known about Charm and the farm, as sure as he was they existed in the shadow, he also knew that his feelings would never be returned. Ever.

Jin almost choked as the knowledge spread through his mind. Lena the Giant would never love him. She didn't feel that way, and that's just who she was. He struggled to breathe, feeling like someone had drop-kicked him right in the heart. He quickly turned away so that the others couldn't see his pain. What was the point of all of this, if Lena would never feel the same as he did? No matter how amazing and awesome he was, she'd never love him.

Wow, these bursts of awareness were definitely getting crueler. At least he also knew that she'd never love Shefin, too, which wasn't much comfort, but it was all he had at the moment.

She doesn't have to be in love with you to like *you, or be your friend. And really, isn't that just as good in a different way? Not to mention that she's a mortal and you're not; maybe that's better anyway?*

Ugh, even without its old voice, his knowledge somehow still managed to be annoying. Right or wrong, this would all have to wait, as he was needed. For now, he'd just ignore this newfound realization and watch over Lena to fulfill the knight's third wish, yes, but also because it just felt wrong not to.

Maybe Lena would never love him. But that didn't mean Jin couldn't still watch over her, protect her, and be her friend.

He shook his head, not liking how his knowledge was making him more rational. *Quit it!* he shouted in his mind, then prepared himself, pushing all his feelings to the side. After all, a bunch of wolves was about to enter an animal farm. He probably should be concentrating on keeping the farmers alive at the moment.

Lena led the now-human-or-close-enough group toward the blue dome, behind which they could see shapes moving, though Jin couldn't make out what they were. That was probably for the best, as he didn't trust Susi or Tala yet. Hopefully, once they were inside the dome, Coni could keep them in line.

"Hello!" Lena shouted out, waving as they reached the magical dome. The shapes on the other side stopped, then approached, getting almost close enough to reveal what sort of creatures they were.

Weirdly, they all looked to be standing upright on two legs. Not that animals couldn't do that, though it still seemed a bit odd.

"What is this?" Jill asked from right up against the dome, the closest of any of them due to her invisibility. "I thought you said they were animals. These people are all human!"

Jin's eyes widened as he realized she was right: as the farmers approached, their shapes *were* clearly human now, without even a trace of pig or cow or whatever other kinds of animals might have been there. What was going on? How could his knowledge be so off?

Though if it was wrong about this, maybe it could be wrong about *Lena*, too?

"Go away," one of the farmers said, his voice muffled by the dome. "You're not going to trick us, shadow."

"We're not the shadow!" Lena shouted, and grabbed Coni's spear from her. The wolf girl shouted out indignantly, but Lena waved the spear around, showing off its glow. "See? The darkness wouldn't be able to make a light like this!"

More farmers had approached the dome, and now Jin could barely make out soft conversations between them. He made his ears larger to better hear, which helped a bit.

"We *can't* let them in," said one of the farmers to another. "They'll be trapped here as well."

Trapped? Uh-oh.

"Isn't that better than leaving them in the shadow?" another said.

"Maybe for now," the first one said. "But think about how they'll feel in a month, a year, a decade. This is for their own good."

What was going on inside that dome? It sounded almost like some kind of prison, the way the farmers were talking. But again, there was nothing in his knowledge about traps, prisons, or anything else. If this was how accurate the cosmic knowledge had been the entire time, no wonder it'd been so useless.

"We just need a place to rest," Jin shouted out. "We won't stay long. We're only traveling through the shadowlands, and need to be on our way as soon as possible."

"Speak for yourself," Tala said quietly, looking a bit too hungry for Jin's taste. "If they have pigs, we might want to stay awhile."

"That's even worse," one of the farmers whispered, just barely loud enough for Jin's enhanced ears to pick up. "They'll be stuck here forever. Don't let them in!"

"We all know that 'in' is better than 'out,' no matter how

terrible it is in here," another farmer said. "I'm calling the pigs."

The *pigs*? Jin blinked in surprise. Wait, so *was* he right about the animals? Why was this farm so confusing?

"Wait one minute," one of the farmers shouted through the dome. "Our bosses will decide if you can come in or not."

Three new shapes appeared farther back inside the farm, then gradually got closer, revealing more *humans*, not pigs. All of this left Jin even more puzzled. Why would they call those humans pigs, if they weren't actually animals? Hopefully it wasn't just an insult.

These new "bosses" spoke to the farmers who'd already gathered by the dome, too far away for Jin to hear. They must have made a choice, though, as a moment later, one of the bosses approached the dome and touched it briefly, then retreated back behind the others.

Instantly, the magical blue light in front of them separated, revealing an entrance just big enough for one person at a time. That didn't exactly make Jin feel much better about this whole thing, considering entering single file certainly made for an easy way to pick the group off, if that was the farmers' intention.

But they didn't *seem* to want to hurt Jin and his friends. If anything, the farmers sounded like they were looking out for them. But what was so dangerous about the farm?

On the other side of the dome, one of the non-boss farmers—a human male, which again was *not* what Jin "knew" should be here—waved for them to enter. "Quickly," he said. "Before the shadow decides to test your light."

"Thank you," Lena said, nodding at the farmer as she carried Rufus (and Shefin, who hid in one of her pockets) inside the dome. Coni and Susi followed behind her, while Tala pushed Jin through next. As soon as Tala came in as well, the dome slammed shut ominously.

As it did, a wave of exhaustion passed over Jin, and he felt faint out of nowhere. Granted, he hadn't stopped to rest recently, at least not since the fairy queens had kidnapped him, so maybe he was just tired. But still, it was odd to come on so suddenly, and so *strongly*.

"I don't like this," Jill said, looking around at the various human farmers, all staring at them with a mix of curiosity and pity. "And it doesn't help that you had bad information. Why did you say they were animals?"

Jin didn't have an answer for her necessarily, so decided to examine the farmers more closely. He peered at the nearest one using his magical senses, then gasped.

"Well hello, newcomers!" said a short, very pink man, one of the three the farmer had called both bosses and pigs. He stepped out from behind the larger group, dressed in some of the finest clothing Jin had ever seen, followed by two other men who must have been his brothers, given how alike they looked and dressed. "Welcome to our farm!"

The other farmers went silent now, looking down at the ground or anywhere but at the boss men. But Jin was beginning to understand why.

They are *pigs!* he thought at Jill. *Well, at least they* were. *Yes, they aren't now, but I can see the remnants of the spell in them. And it's not just them: All of the farmers were animals: I'm seeing former cows, horses, even chickens. But I think they had their curses removed somehow?*

"Thank you for letting us in," Lena said, bowing her head respectfully to the three former pigs. "We won't be any trouble. All we need is a safe place to rest for a bit, and we'll be on our way."

"On your way?" one of the pig men said, sounding confused. "But you're making use of our magical dome, aren't you? And that requires payment. No, I'm afraid no one's going anywhere until you've paid what you now owe us."

"For a few hours rest, we'll need a full day's work," the second pig man said. "Unfortunately, to do that, you'll need to pay for a day's worth of dome usage, as well, which will cost a *week* of work."

Susi growled, but Coni raised a hand to stop her sister from doing anything. "We didn't know there'd be a price," the wolf girl said. "We'll just be leaving, then."

"Oh, you can't leave," the third pig man said, as the other two grinned smugly. "You've already made use of some dome time, so the debt has already started. And *no one* leaves until they pay their debts, plus interest. So you better get used to things here on the farm, as you'll be here for a long, *long* time!"

CHAPTER 27

The moment Lena walked inside the dome, her whole body went weak, like she hadn't eaten anything, or gotten enough sleep. But without knowing the cause and not wanting to let on that she could barely stand, she'd tried her best to hide it when they'd first entered.

Now, after hearing the three well-dressed men basically claim they were prisoners, her anger restored some of her energy. There was no time for this, not with the shadow spreading to the Cursed City!

"We never agreed to any of that," she said, trying to stay calmer this time but not finding it easy.

"Who says you have to?" one of the pink men said. "You're making use of our protection, and you're going to pay for that privilege." He snapped his fingers, and two extremely large men stepped forward from where they'd been waiting just behind the three pink men. "Papa, we have some dishonest new farmers. They're trying to take something that doesn't belong to them without paying. How about you introduce them to something we call 'integrity,' and help them pay their debts?"

Lena's eyes widened at the man's words, even as the one who the pink man called Papa stepped forward, a grin spreading over his face. "Happy to," Papa growled, and put a hand on Lena's shoulder.

She immediately tried removing that hand, but unfortunately, when her arm hit Papa's, it came to a crashing halt, sending pain shooting all the way up to her shoulder.

"Ow!" she shouted, clutching her arm in surprise. What was going on? Even a large man shouldn't be anywhere near this strong, not compared to her giant strength.

"Um, Coni?" Susi said, looking far less sure of herself than usual. "I can't change."

"Neither can I!" Tala shouted, and immediately turned her spear on the three pink men. *What are you doing to us?*

"We aren't doing *anything*," the pink man said, smiling smugly. "It's the dome. Our great-grandparents were cursed by a wizard, turned into animals to act as the wizards' familiars.

But when they escaped, they stole this magic from the wizard without even knowing what it did. When the shadow reached these lands, we'd already set up the farm here with a bunch of other animal familiars, hoping to hide from the wizards. We didn't want to lose everything we'd worked hard to build, so we threw everything we could at the darkness. Turns out the dome not only absorbs the shadow's magic, but also works wonders on curses and such. Just temporary at first, of course, but the longer you're here, the more permanent the change becomes."

"You're welcome for ending all of your curses, by the way," said another of the pink men. "We all used to be like you, changed by shadow magic. My brothers and I were *pigs*, if you can believe it! But once we realized the dome could absorb magic, we cured all our fellow animal farmers, since we were all victims of a magician's curse. Not that we did it for free, mind you. We're not gullible. Our ancestors passed along this valuable gift, and we'd be suckers not to charge what it's worth!"

"Speaking of," said the third pink man, "I'm afraid now we'll have to add a 'cured curses' cost on to what you owe us, as well."

Coni roared in anger and stabbed forward with her spear, only for Papa to grab it and yank it out of her hands. The other large man stepped forward and took both the remaining spears from a shocked Susi and Tala.

"I feel so *weak*," Susi said, and began to sway.

"You'll get used to it," the third pink man said, grinning as well. "Everyone feels that way at first, but it'll get easier. Still, every hour you don't work means you owe us double, so I'd make sure you don't rest too long."

"Just do what they say," one of the other farmers whispered to Lena. "At least they keep us safe from the shadow."

"I don't care what they keep you safe from!" Lena shouted, though even that much effort sent spots bursting in front of her eyes. "This is *wrong*. Why would they charge you to keep you safe? Doesn't the dome do that by itself?"

"It does," one of the pink men said, shrugging. "But since it's *ours*, we decide who gets to stay inside it."

"And if our farmers object, we can always shut it down everywhere but our house," the second one said, pointing behind him at a large brick building that towered over the rest of the farm, as every other structure was made from either hay or wood, and much shorter.

"And then we'll see how they enjoy living in the darkness," the third pink man said with a laugh.

"They'll work," a second farmer said, throwing a warning look at Lena. "Because they know if they don't, then we'll *all* suffer for it."

Lena started to respond but couldn't think of what to say to that. This was all so wrong! How could the pink men be treating the others like this? It was just so evil, honestly. But how could they fix this, help these farmers, or even escape themselves? They'd have to fight, even in their weakened state, and . . .

And she *couldn't* fight. This was the Trial of Warfare, it had to be. The fairy queens said she'd have to resist the urge to fight, to stay peaceful.

But then they'd be trapped here, with no way to stop the shadow! How would letting the entire world be covered by darkness somehow make her more worthy?

"Come on, time to get started," Papa said, and his partner grunted. They circled around behind Lena and her friends, then pushed them forward, making both Susi and Coni stumble, and almost knocking Lena off her feet. She managed not to fall with Jin's quick help and looked up at the genie gratefully.

"I feel so weak," she whispered to him as Papa and his friend pushed them farther into the dome. "What is this dome?"

Jin looked up at it, then closed his eyes. "Whoa, dizzy," he said, sounding dazed. "It's um . . . it's *something*, for sure. That much I know."

Okay, so apparently Jin was *also* affected, maybe even worse than Lena was, considering she could still think straight at least. But without Jin's magic, they really didn't have any other choice but to fight.

And then she'd lose the Trial of Warfare.

"Keep moving," Papa said. "Junior here and I will carry you if we have to. You'll learn soon enough to pay what you owe. After all, nothing makes you more honest than a hard days' work."

Lena almost laughed at how ridiculous Papa's words were. How did *work* make someone honest? The other farmers seemed annoyed by this too, but kept it to themselves, fearing the pigs. But the farmers had the numbers to resist, to shut down the pigs, if they were willing to take the chance. Maybe that was the way out of this, the way to pass the trial while also fixing this injustice?

"Um," said a voice from Lena's pocket, startling her. "I think we might have a problem."

Shefin? She'd almost forgotten about the boy. She glanced down at her pocket where he'd been hiding, only to find he'd *grown*. He'd scrunched himself down as much as possible, but even from above, Lena could see that the pocket was straining not to break completely, and half of Shefin was already hanging out of it.

Without another word, Lena tried to pull him from the pocket, hoping to hide him behind Rufus in her arms. But she misjudged how heavy he was now, or how weak she'd become, as she found him much harder to lift than she'd expected.

Trying again, she managed to swing him up and tuck him into her other arm, mostly hidden by Rufus's fur. At least whatever the dome was doing hadn't touched her cat, as he hadn't returned to normal yet.

Except this *was* his original size already. He'd been big so long that she'd almost forgotten the Cauldron of Truth had grown him this large. Did that mean . . . ?

Her fingers fumbling from nervousness, she undid his collar and pulled it off with her free hand. Just as she'd feared, Rufus didn't change size. Instead, he just looked up at her and meowed.

"It's sapping *all* of our magic, not just the shadow!" Shefin whispered from below her. "Either that, or we're all made from the darkness like giants are. That's a horrifying thought. We need to get out of here, Lena, or we're all going to be a lot more human than we'd expected!"

Ice ran down Lena's spine as she realized he was right. But Shefin's words also made her aware that there was a more immediate concern to worry about, trial or no trial.

"Jin is *made* of magic," she whispered to Shefin as they approached what looked like a massive tool shed, open and filled with all kinds of farming instruments. The fields were just beyond the shed, and dozens of farmers were already working there, digging up the dirt or planting seeds. "We have to get him out of here, *now*."

"Okay, and how do you plan on doing that?" Shefin asked, then ducked behind Rufus as Papa moved around to face them.

"You three will plow the fields," he said, pointing at the wolf sisters, who were now leaning against each other in an effort to stand up. "The rest of you are planters. I want to see these fields tilled and seeded by sundown, or you'll work through the night until you're done." He pointed at three fields grown over with weeds, and without a single worker in them.

"That's impossible," Lena said to him. "Half of us can barely stand. There's no way we'll finish this tonight."

"Best *get to work*, then," Papa said with a big smile, and threw a bag of seeds at Lena. It hit her hard enough to almost knock her down, and she barely managed to keep ahold of Rufus and Shefin.

"I'm starting to think this farm isn't so great," Shefin said, rolling his eyes. "What it really needs is some sort of iron fist to rule it."

Lena blinked, then blinked again. "You know what?" she said. "Maybe it's not too late for you to join in a revolution. I've got an idea."

CHAPTER 28

et to work. That's what the man had said, right? Jin could barely keep the thought in his head as he stumbled along behind Lena, struggling to just hold his bag of seeds. At this rate, he wasn't going to be able to stand much longer, let alone do any farming. Part of him wondered if he should let his physical body go, to save that energy and turn insubstantial.

But if he did, would he have enough magic to bring it back later? Or would it even matter, with the way the dome seemed to be absorbing his power?

"I've got an idea on how we can get out of here *and* help the farmers," Lena whispered as she glanced over her shoulder at him, looking really worried. "I hate to ask, but we could really use your help. But only if it doesn't put you in danger. I'm not risking your life, no matter what."

Her concern made him smile and gave him enough energy to respond. "Always," he said, trying to look cool and unaffected, only for the world to spin around him. Lena grabbed his shoulder to keep him from collapsing, which again made him feel a bit better. "What do you need?"

"He's fading fast," Shefin said from Lena's arms, though he was quickly growing large enough that she wouldn't be able to hide him soon. Eventually he'd even be Lena's size. Well, a foot shorter, maybe. He did seem a little small, even for a Lilliputian. Jin smiled at that, wondering if there were even *tinier* Lilliputians out there. Would the babies be the size of one of Jin's knuckles? Would—

He bumped into Lena, who had stopped short, whispering over and over with Shefin. "Sorry," he murmured, his eyelids drooping as he stared at her in confusion. "Did something . . . happen?"

She looked at him again for a moment, frowned, then turned back to Shefin. "You can do this, Shefin. Don't worry about Thomas or anyone else. Prove it to yourself. *This* is your revolution."

Revolution? What was going on, other than "revolution" being a fun word?

"I taught those rebels everything they know, trust me," Shefin said, and winked at her. Jin glared at him for that, but Lena just sighed and nodded.

"Just keep it *peaceful*," she said. "No fighting. If the farmers unite as a group, we can fix all of this without anyone getting hurt."

"Sure, whatever you say," the Lilliputian boy said with a grin, then turned to Jin. "Genie, I need your help here. Can you make it so everyone inside the dome can hear my voice? I don't care how, or if the boss people overhear. If this works, it shouldn't matter."

Jin blinked, not following. *Could* he do that? He probably had enough magic left, yes, but that would be it. If he cast that spell, and they still couldn't escape the dome, he'd be done for.

Not that he had much of a chance as it was. Ugh.

Selflessness is the worst, he thought. But was being selfish any better? The pigs here were taking advantage of all the other farmers just because they'd been left this dome by their parents' parents. They were maybe the *most* selfish creatures he'd ever met, and while part of Jin admired how foolproof their plan was, look at the pain it caused. Look at how miserable the farmers were, *Lena* was. Look at— Was that a bird? What a pretty bird! He should tell Jill.

Wait. Where *was* Jill? Right, he'd only ever been able to sense her due to his magic. And with that going, he couldn't even hear her, let alone see her. She'd be gone for good, or maybe even absorbed by the magic herself.

All because of the pigs' selfishness.

Maybe there *was* something to be said for selflessness after all.

"Ready?" Shefin asked, and Jin sighed, then nodded. If only the cosmic knowledge were here to see how giving he was being. He lifted one shaky hand, then cast a spell to raise the volume of Shefin's voice as loudly as he could.

Even using that little magic forced Jin to his knees, and he felt much weaker than before. Whatever the Lilliputian planned, he hoped the boy did it quick.

"People of the farm!" Shefin shouted, and Jin saw Lena cover her ears, wincing in agony. The loud sound of Shefin's voice must be painful to her, though Jin couldn't feel anything. Probably not a great sign, that. "Listen to me. Your bosses have you trapped here, tilling their fields and growing their food, all while they sit back and reap the benefits. And why? Because their grandparents stole the magic of the dome.

The pigs didn't even make it *themselves*, let alone work for it!"

The farmers around them paused in their work and turned to stare at Shefin.

So did Papa and his son, the two enormously large men who Jin sensed used to be bears. They were certainly the *size* of bears, if nothing else. And unfortunately, they were already coming over.

"No one's against honest work," Shefin continued. "But that's not what this is. They're taking advantage of you, making up unfair rules to keep you stuck here working for them forever. And they use Papa and Junior to scare you, keep you intimidated, because they're terrified you might realize that none of this is right! They're scared you'll realize you outnumber them, and could shut this all down at any time. You could even take the dome's magic back for yourselves!"

"Shut your mouth or I'll throw you out into the shadow myself!" Papa yelled, now jogging toward them, his son just behind.

A few of the farmers moved to intercept the two enforcers, but Papa barreled right through them, even as Shefin started looking a bit more nervous.

"All we have to do is work together, for *ourselves* instead of the bosses!" the Lilliputian yelled, backing away a bit. "Let the bosses work at our side, earning their safety just like we do. Wouldn't that be more fair? More right?"

Papa let out a huge growl and leapt directly at Shefin, a bear of a man soaring straight at the still-small Lilliputian. Shefin shouted in surprise and horror, throwing his arms up to block him . . .

But something collided with Papa, knocking him to the side, just barely missing Shefin. Jin glanced up and found Lena standing over the Lilliputian, her fists clenched and a look of horror on her face. "I couldn't let him . . . I couldn't . . . *no,* no no no! Give me another chance—I can do it, I swear!" she screamed in horror.

"Lena?" Jin whispered, reaching out a hand to help if he could, but there was just no strength left. He collapsed back to the ground, everything going completely black now, all his concentration wrapped up in Shefin's voice enhancement. The spell wouldn't last much longer, but he'd do his best for as long as he could.

"Jin?" he heard Lena say, but her voice came from what sounded like miles away. "Jin! Are you okay?"

"Get your hands off me!" Papa shouted, and Jin heard grunts and shouts from where the man had landed. But worrying about what was happening seemed to take so much energy, and wouldn't it be easier to just rest?

The darkness around him didn't feel so scary now, somehow. No, it almost reminded him of another time, a time before he'd woken in this world, surprised and startled, with only his cosmic knowledge to guide him. It was a world that . . .

A world that was *moving*, strangely. Or so it looked from what little light Jin could still see.

A bright blue light filled his vision, and for a moment, Jin felt like he was on fire, being pulled in multiple directions at once. He screamed in pain and fear, as did someone else, someone he knew . . . but then the light faded just as fast as it'd appeared, and the blackness returned.

Except it wasn't the same darkness he'd seen a moment ago, when he'd been so exhausted, so close to death. And somehow, he actually didn't feel quite so weak anymore, either. What had just happened? Where was he?

He looked up, still weak, and found Lena holding him in her arms. He felt her tremble beneath him, and suddenly he began to realize what she'd done.

They were outside the dome. She'd carried him out, and in doing so, saved his life

And also exposed herself to the waiting shadow.

JIN, it said in his mind. *THIS IS WHAT THE HUMANS*

DO. *THEY HURT YOU, STEAL YOUR POWER, ALL BECAUSE THEY ARE SCARED. JOIN ME, AND YOU'LL HAVE THE MAGIC TO WIPE THEM FROM THIS WORLD!*

He shook his head, not sure he could even respond to the shadow's offer. "Lena," he tried to say, but almost choked, his throat felt so frail. "Lena. Go back . . . *inside.*"

"No," she whispered, and Jin started to see, to *feel* the shadow around them get closer, writhing in happiness at new victims. "I'll . . . protect you. I don't know how, but I'll find a way. I might have . . . have *failed* at everything else, but I'm not letting the shadow take *you,* too!"

Her words gave him energy again, but it wouldn't be enough, not to hold off the shadow. He raised his hand, hoping maybe a light spell would buy them some time, but even that fizzled out immediately.

THEY WILL ALWAYS CUT YOU DOWN, FORCE YOU TO SERVE THEM. BUT I OFFER YOU STRENGTH, THE POWER TO FIGHT BACK. TAKE IT, DJINN, AND TOGETHER WE WILL BE UNSTOPPABLE!

And then the shadow took hold of Jin, and he screamed as it filled him with its darkness.

CHAPTER 29

As the shadow flowed over Jin, absorbing into his skin, Lena felt her last bit of hope start to fade away, leaving an emptiness behind like nothing she'd ever felt. *"NO!"* she shouted, frantically trying to pull him back toward the dome. She'd already failed the world, but she couldn't, she *wouldn't* lose Jin, too!

Even if she managed to get him inside the farm's dome again, though, would that really be any better? Another few minutes beneath it might kill him.

The shadow reached for her, and her whole body went ice-cold as she realized she was about to lose herself to the darkness as well. But still she held tight to the genie, not letting him go, not willing to lose anyone else.

Her own strength was slowly returning here outside the dome, but not fast enough. And it wouldn't matter anyway, not without the Illumination of Worthiness. Without the candle's flame, she couldn't fight the shadow, no matter how strong she was.

But *maybe* she could delay it until Jin's strength returned? She grabbed a broken branch on the ground and swung it at the darkness connected to Jin, only for the shadow to separate and allow the branch to pass through it unhindered.

"You've failed your first two trials," said a familiar voice from the darkness, and the shadow formed into a version of the head fairy queen. Another quickly formed as well, then another, until all eleven shadow fairy queens surrounded her in a half circle. "You have proven yourself *very* unworthy, child."

"I'm sorry, I'm so sorry!" she shouted, tears running down her face now as she slowly tried to drag Jin back toward the farm. But the shadow yanked on the genie, throwing Lena forward, just short of the dark fairy queens. She caught herself at the last moment, but it was too late: Jin disappeared into the shadow completely now, leaving her alone in the darkness.

Something broke in Lena's mind, and rage poured over her like a wave. "You can't have him!" she roared, and punched the ground as hard as she could. The blow sent mild tremors through the woods and the farm both.

The shadow fairy queens just sneered.

"You still revel in your own darkness, don't you?" the shadows said. "This is why you've lost, young giant. You don't *want* to be worthy. The evil inside has a hold of you, and you won't let it go."

"Please, give him back!" she cried, falling to her knees now. "You don't even want him. You want me; *I'm* the one made of shadow! Take me, and let Jin go!"

The shadow fairy queens slowly smiled, all in unison. "You think we want *you*? The genie's magic is all we are after. You are just an afterthought, little giant, no one important. We will take you, as the king demands, but the genie was *always* the one we were after."

Lena's mouth dropped open, not understanding. The shadow wanted Jin, not her? "But I thought you . . . you created the giants!"

"Yes, we did," the fairy queens said, and now the shadow spoke from all eleven mouths at the same time. "But what little remains of our magic inside you is too weak to matter. If it were up to us, we'd let you go on to your third trial, just to watch you fail once more."

Lena's eyes widened, and she started to feel a glimmer of

hope. "It's not too late? I can still prove myself worthy if I pass the last trial?"

The shadowy fairy queens laughed, flooding Lena with despair. "You could not hold your anger in the Trial of Wrath. You could not resist fighting in the Trial of Warfare. What makes you think you could resist your own wickedness?"

Their words felt like a knife going into Lena's stomach, and she doubled over. "I tried . . . to do what was right," she whispered. "I couldn't let Shefin be hurt. And maybe I did get angry, but I only used it to help, not destroy. I did try, I swear!"

"Did you? Or was the darkness inside you too precious to rise above?" the fairy queens asked. "Do not worry, young giant. Your kind was born of shadow. It is your *destiny* to fall to your love of destruction."

"Noooo," Lena wailed, shaking her head, not wanting to believe it. But the shadow wasn't wrong. She *had* failed, in exactly the ways the trial was testing, no matter the reasons. But there was still the last trial, the Trial of Wickedness . . . she could still prove herself, if the Illumination of Worthiness would let her—

"Would you like to know what the third trial would have been?" the fairy queens asked.

"You don't . . . you don't know," Lena whispered as the shadow tendrils slithered in closer. "You're not the *real* fairy queens. You *can't* know."

"Ah, but we have your genie now, and he knows *everything*," the shadowy fairy queens said, continuing to strike at her worst fears. "Perhaps he could have helped, if he'd only realized what power he had. The Trial of Wickedness would have taken place in the last oasis in the shadow, a goblin town, exiles from Charm. And yet, they themselves have found the light, child, in ways you never would. For they have *chosen* to leave their monstrous origins behind. They have converted themselves to humanity, by their own choice, using magic from Pan the satyr."

"*Converted?*" Lena croaked, her mouth almost too dry to speak. "What do you mean?"

"They, like you, are the product of shadow," the fairy queens said. "But they chose to rise above it, to follow a path of goodness, of light, of *humanity*, as they once were before the darkness, as you *all* were, in ages past! Yes, their bodies remain monstrous, but their minds are now good and pure, for they have rejected the ways of the darkness, and become worthy. And all it took was a *choice*. A choice to no longer be wicked, to no longer be ruled by their own impulses. A choice to become *human.* All it took was a magic spell to overwrite their very natures, making them believe they are something *better,* and therefore leaving all aspects of the shadow behind."

Lena's mouth opened and closed, but she couldn't find the words. The goblins *chose* to become something new, because they saw themselves as unworthy, as lesser, as *evil?* And to be good, to be pure, they had to be . . . human?

"That can't *be,*" she whispered, her throat so tight it almost cut off her breath. Disgust and nausea filled her stomach, but from somewhere deep, she found the strength to push to her feet. The fairy queens responded, but her heart was beating so loudly she almost couldn't hear them over it. "That's . . . that's *wrong.*"

"You hear, child, but you don't *listen,*" the shadow said. "The goblins were born wrong, but overcame that when they chose to become human. You couldn't follow their lead, though, could you, child? You would have chosen to stay as you are, a product of darkness, and thereby proven yourself unworthy."

Lena slowly reached into her endless pouch and retrieved the Illumination of Worthiness. She held it up, knowing it wouldn't light, but not able to help herself.

The candle didn't find her worthy . . . because she wasn't human? That's what the trials had all been about? Not just that giants or goblins or any other magic-infused creature had been made by the shadow, but that they weren't human?

And without that, the candle wouldn't think she was good enough?

Clenching her fist, Lena broke the Illumination of Worthiness in two, then dropped both halves to the ground as she turned to face the shadow.

"Again, you fall back on your destructive instincts!" The shadow fairy queens laughed. "Look at you, giant! You're just as much a monster as everyone thinks! And now you've thrown away the one weapon you had against the darkness!"

Lena shook her head, then raised her hands up like a boxer. "That was never going to help. Not me. Because I am Lena the Giant." She cracked her knuckles. "And giants fight . . . to show their *might*."

"You can't defeat the shadow, not without the candle," the fairy queens sneered. "What do you intend to do, strike us down with your fists? We will take you over at the first touch!"

"I will fight, yes," Lena continued, taking a step closer to the shadow. Weirdly, the tendrils of darkness closest to her seemed to retreat from her, just a little, and it brought a smile to her face, in spite of everything. "But I don't fight to hurt people, or to destroy. I'm going to use my strength to fight for something *better*. To protect anyone who needs it, and make right things that are wrong. Like this farm. Like the city of Charm. Like this whole sick *game* of the fairy queens!"

"You know not what you speak," the fairy queens said, merging their shadows back into one. "That strength is *wrong*. *You* are wrong! And you refuse to be right!"

Lena almost laughed at that. "You took it too far, shadow. You, the fairy queens, their whole horrible story . . . I was almost believing it. You just about had me thinking I really was all that you say. But to wipe away all that I am to be human, just because that's the fairy queens' definition of worthy? Those poor goblins! They must have felt so disgusted with their true selves to choose to convert. I can't imagine anything worse, and when this is over, I hope I can help them."

"This *is* over, and you've lost!" the fairy queen sneered, and her shadowy arms came flying at Lena. Instead of dodging or retreating, though, Lena grabbed for the darkness and held it tight, even as it flowed into her, making her skin go pale and cold.

"The only thing that's over is the fairy queens' story," she said quietly as the shadow stared at her in shock, even as it slowly absorbed her. "Right here, right now, we're going to start a new one."

"And what's that?" the shadow asked, sounding far less sure of itself now.

A bright light came flying out of nowhere and cut right through the shadow's arms, releasing Lena and making the fairy queen howl in agony. Lena glanced back to find Coni standing just outside the dome. The wolf sister smiled at her, then pushed back inside, where Lena thought she could hear cheering, of all things. She smiled as well, then turned back to the shadow and picked up Coni's spear from where it had hit the ground.

"The story of Lena the Giant realizing she's *just fine who she is,*" Lena said, still smiling, then leapt straight at the shadows, her spear bright as the sun.

CHAPTER 30

in had felt this same sense of anger and hate before. He again recognized the voice, the rage of it now, from when he'd touched the Spark and temporarily absorbed its power.

But now, with the addition of his knowledge, he knew what it actually *was*.

"I *know* you," he said to the darkness all around him, swirling within his mind. "I know who you are now. And I know what you want!"

I WANT WHAT *YOU* WANT, the shadow shouted, making Jin wince at the volume. I WANT TO LIVE FREE FROM THOSE WHO HAVE IMPRISONED ME, AND FOR THOSE JAILERS TO SUFFER. I WANT TO RID CREATION OF ALL WHO WOULD OPPOSE ME!

"Well first, there's no need to yell, okay?" he said. "Also, we could have just talked about this all back in the physical plane. You didn't need to pull me here."

THE GIRL. THE GIANT GIRL. SHE WON'T LET ME HAVE YOU. SHE HAS NOT STOPPED TRYING TO STEAL YOU AWAY. *I WILL NOT LET THAT HAPPEN!*

Jin's eyes widened. Lena was trying to save him, even now that the shadow had absorbed him? The thought gave him strength, but also filled him with anxious worry for the giant girl and rage that she was in danger. "Don't you *dare* touch her! If you do, I don't care what you want from me. I'll make sure you *never* get it, as long as I live. *Do you understand me?*"

YOU WOULD DEFY ME? I WILL KEEP YOU HERE AS LONG AS I WISH—

"No," Jin said, "you *won't*. If you want me to continue to even *think* about listening to you, then you will *not* try to take over Lena's mind. Promise me you won't infect her." He glared all around him. *"Promise me."*

The shadow seemed to exhale in a sort of annoyed sigh. I CANNOT. I *MUST* DO AS I AM ORDERED. I HAVE NO CHOICE. HOWEVER, I HAVE SO FAR BEEN . . .

UNSUCCESSFUL IN CAPTURING THE GIANT GIRL, IN SPITE OF USING HER FEARS AGAINST HER—

"Oh, that won't work," Jin said, his anger slowly fading. "Because as much as she doubts herself, mostly thanks to you and the fairy queens, Lena isn't ever worried for herself. Just other people. Because she's *just that great* a person." He crossed his arms. "But it sounds like the first thing we need to fix is the king's control over you, so you can stop doing all of *this*." He waved his hands around. "Even without him forcing you to take over the land, you have to know you're going about this all wrong. You're just playing into the hands of those that hate you."

The shadow began rumbling all around him, as if it could barely hold back its anger. Which was probably the case. THEY DID THIS TO ME! ANYTHING I DO NOW IS TO DESTORY THEM, ALONG WITH THE REST OF THIS WORLD. I WILL TEAR DOWN EVERYTHING THEY HOLD DEAR!

"Yeah, no, I get it," Jin said, still wishing the shadow would just quiet down a bit. "They imprisoned you. They named you shadow, darkness, *evil*. And then when you were released, they knew you would be angry and so set about rampaging out in the world, proving them right. You fell right into the story they were already telling about you. I understand why, but it's not helping anything."

The shadow hissed in rage, then let out a scream of primal anger that almost made Jin nervous. He looked down to find his hands trembling slightly and realized it wasn't just "almost."

YOU DARE SPEAK TO ME LIKE THIS?!

"I do dare," Jin said, trying to hide the worry in his voice. Yes, the shadow wanted something from him, but it was still far more powerful than he was, even if he had all his magic, which he still didn't, thanks to another thousand years or so of servitude. Maybe making it angrier wasn't helping. "Because you have to see how they work! I'm not saying your anger, this rage, isn't justified, because it completely is. In fact, if I were you, I'd have already burned this world to ash, probably. But that's not how you're going to beat them. There are other ways. *Better* ways."

YES. I WILL BEAT THEM WITH YOUR HELP. TOGETHER, YOU WILL GIVE FORM TO MY RIGHTEOUS ANGER, AND WE WILL *END* THIS INJUSTICE PUT UPON ME BY THE—

"Whoa, hey, I never said I'd help you!" Jin pointed out, then braced himself as the shadow let out another wail of rage. "I mean, I didn't say I wouldn't, either, but I need to see if you can hold up your end of the bargain, first. Show me Lena."

For a moment, Jin wondered if he'd gone too far. But then an image appeared next to him, Lena fighting a fairy queen made of shadow with one of the wolves' spears.

And what's more, she was smiling.

Jin couldn't help grinning too, and not just because he enjoyed watching her destroy the shadowy fairy queens. "I knew you'd make the right choice," he said quietly, then raised his voice to address the shadow. "Good! That's the first step in establishing trust, proving that you can keep your word. At least, that's what the cosmic knowledge used to tell me. But now I've got everything he knew, all up in here." He tapped his head, then paused. "Wait a second . . . does that mean the cosmic knowledge's voice was just *me* all along? It was, wasn't it! Why would I be so *mean* to me?"

IT TOOK YOU THIS LONG TO REALIZE THAT?

"All right, lay off it!" Jin shouted, annoyed now too. "Don't take your anger out on me. I'm trying to help you." He paused, considering things. "But if the fairy-queen spell released the inhibitions on my knowledge . . . *oh*, I get it. *Oh*. That's . . . *oh!*"

YOU BEGIN TO SEE THE DEPTHS THEY WOULD GO TO NOW, DON'T YOU?

"I mean, I'd like to think I'm *always* ready to see the depths people would go to, but yes, you're right. I'm a little surprised." That wasn't really giving himself enough credit, though. It wasn't like he *knew* the cosmic knowledge had been restricted from telling him everything by the ones who'd kept Jin from accessing the knowledge in the first place. And while it had claimed that was due to the elder ifrits, Jin now knew it had lied about that.

His own knowledge, lying to him, without him even knowing it. They *were* good.

"Our enemies have planned ahead," he said finally. "*Way* ahead, in fact. So to beat them, we're going to need to plan ahead too. You know, trap them. Be . . . *subtle*."

WE NEED TO DESTROY THEM, WIPE THEM OFF THE FACE OF THIS PLANET.

"That's not the subtle I was thinking of," Jin said. "But I like your spirit."

I ENJOY YOUR PRESENCE AS WELL, LITTLE DJINN.

Aww! The shadow wasn't actually that bad, once you got to know it. Its fear magic was pretty awful, okay, but it was only obeying its master's orders, just like Jin did when fulfilling his wishes. And yes, it had every right in the world to be angry, but if Jin could work with it, use its power to help free the darkness from its servitude, that'd at least begin to fix things.

Not to mention that it might help the shadow's mood, too, honestly.

"Can I ask you a question, before launching into the plan?" he said.

YOU JUST DID.

Jin rolled his eyes. "Why did your magic create the giants, the ogres, all those things? You've been changing things out in the world, every time you've been released into it. Why? Why did that happen? I'm sure you were never *ordered* to make humans into creatures like that."

YOU KNOW WHY, LITTLE DJINN.

Jin supposed he did. "Because chaos magic is all about change," he said finally, nodding in understanding. "And genies are *made* of chaos magic."

THAT WE ARE, said the shadow, though Jin supposed he should stop calling it that. Shadow was the name the fairy queens had given it, in order to scare humans. But it wasn't darkness, it wasn't evil, and it *wasn't* shadow.

"What should I call you?" he asked. "I'm not going to use the fairy queens' name for you any longer."

MARID, said the ifrit. MY NAME IS *MARID*.

CHAPTER 31

I can't believe I fell for all of this!" Lena shouted as she slammed the light spear into the shadowy fairy queen. It disappeared in a scream of pain, only to be replaced by another, and another. "I should have known from the beginning. *No one* is born bad; I don't care what kind of creature they are. And just because I'm strong and like to fight does *not* make me evil. I like to fight to keep my friends and family safe, and to stop people like you, who would call them unworthy for being who they are!"

She knew that these shadows weren't actually the fairy queens and were instead just representations of what she feared, but she couldn't deny it still felt good to yell at them just the same. Not to mention getting to hit them with the glowing spear.

"You were not *worthy* of our story!" one of the fairy queens shouted, only to yelp in surprise and leap backward as Lena swept her weapon out toward her. Another few fairy queens formed from the shadows behind her, but Lena swung the spear around in a circle, giving herself some room. "We needed a hero, but you were never more than a monstrous failure!"

Lena laughed at how ridiculous they sounded now, then ran her light through that fairy queen, sending her screaming into the darkness. "All this time, you had me going. *Giants are made from evil magic; you have to rise above your base instincts.*" She stabbed another shadow through its leg, and it disappeared as well, only to be replaced by dozens more. "You really did have me believing it!"

"Because it's *true*," another fairy queen shouted. "You could have been someone worthy, if only you'd listened to us!"

Lena took particular delight in sending that fairy queen away. "People like you will *never* think I'm worth anything. Because you can't see past where I come from," she said, not able to stop grinning now. "I should have realized this a long time ago, but the only person who gets to judge me worthy is *me*."

After all the darkness, all the terrible things she'd gone through since her family's visit . . . she couldn't help but feel *free*, now that she'd seen through it all.

Because finally, *finally*, she understood what was happening. The fairy queens hadn't wanted Lena to rise above her giantness. They wanted her to be human.

No, that wasn't it. They wanted her to *want* to be human. But how could anyone believe that humans were automatically better? They were just as capable of making mistakes or being selfish as any "monster." Just in the last day, Lena had met some of the most evil creatures she could have imagined, and they were *all* human. Some of them had even had their shadow magic removed, and somehow were still more of a monster than any giant Lena knew, with the exception of King Denir.

Maybe the shadow *was* evil. Lena honestly didn't know for sure, but why would it even matter? Because the shadow hadn't made Lena: she came from her loving giant parents. The shadow hadn't given Lena her personality, or told her what things to like, or how much to enjoy something. That had been *all* Lena herself.

And now Lena, *herself*, was having a great time fighting the darkness.

"This very act shows that you're just as much a monster as the others!" one fairy queen shouted, right before Lena sent it away with the spear.

"What you call monsters are just people, too, and worthy of our respect!" she shouted, driving her spear through one shadowy fairy queen after another. "The goblins, ogres, orcs, trolls, humans, and *giants*, all matter and are important! Because *we* don't have to change just because we're different. And *we* don't have to become something we're not just to make you less afraid of us!"

"And yet you're reveling in this," one of the shadows sneered. "Look at you! Enjoying the violence, delighting in hating us!"

She whirled around to find the fairy queen who'd spoken, then reached out and grabbed it by the shadow's fake gown. The darkness flowed over her fingers, absorbing into her, but she didn't care. Instead, she looked the shadow right in the eye and smiled.

Then she tore the shadow apart.

"You're right—I did enjoy that," she said as the darkness slipped away from her fingers, re-forming back into itself. And she really was having fun. But it wasn't going to last; she knew that for certain. Because she was absolutely *surrounded* by darkness and wasn't actually hurting it, beyond the temporary pain she inflicted any time she stabbed it with the light spear. That didn't ultimately hurt the shadow, as it just pulled itself back together again, re-forming each and every time.

But her spear would eventually run out of magic, and then . . .

"You've doomed the entire *world* with your selfishness," another fairy queen spat, and before Lena could get to it, a third one appeared.

"The Golden King will *win*, and everyone will suffer, no matter what you say," said this new fairy queen as more and more appeared, threatening to overwhelm her now with sheer numbers. She swung her spear in a circle again, then again, each time hitting a few, but more just took their places.

"Maybe the Golden King *will* spread this shadow over the world," Lena told it. "But before that happens, I'm going to take my friend back, pull Jin out of this horrible darkness, and we're *still* going to fix all of this, no matter what it takes. And you want to know why?"

The fairy queens hissed and attacked as one, flying toward her from all directions . . .

Only for two more light spears to split their darkness in two.

"Because giant girl is *fun*, and we like her just the way she is," Susi said simply, then howled and leapt at the shadows, grabbing one of the spears on her way. Tala did the same from

Lena's other side, while Coni pulled Lena backward, away from the darkness.

"Come on, now's your chance," the wolf girl told her. "Your little friend pulled it off. The farm is ours!"

Lena just shook her head. "Jin's still in there! I'm not leaving until I get him back."

Coni considered this, then shrugged. "Sounds good to me! The light spears won't last much longer, but I've always been curious to see exactly what the darkness does if it takes you over. Might as well find out!"

On *that* optimistic note, Coni transformed into a wolf and leapt at the shadow as well, with Lena right behind her, holding the girl's spear still. After having been pushed back by the wolves' sudden appearance, the darkness had already regrouped and was threatening to overwhelm Coni's two sisters.

And there was still no sign of *Jin*! No matter how far they managed to push into the darkness, there wasn't even a hint of the genie, and Lena began to worry that the shadow magic's claim that it had absorbed him might not have been about scaring her.

What if Jin was now a part of the shadow? What if they couldn't get him out? What if—

"All right, enough!" shouted a familiar voice, and the darkness abruptly froze in place. Before Lena even recognized what was happening, the shadow began to swirl around her and the wolves, as if they were trapped in the eye of a tornado. Faster and faster it whirled, rising up as it turned, growing into something new, no longer multiple fairy queens, but just one creature now, a creature who started to look awfully familiar—

"Jin?" Lena said, not daring to even hope. After all, it could be a version of Jin taken over by the shadow, or even the shadow using his form to strike back against them. She'd still fight it, even in Jin's shape, but it wouldn't be easy *or* pleasant.

"Oh, it's me, don't worry!" Jin said as the darkness continued to pour straight into him. As it did, the shadows slowly fell from his face and body, leaving behind the real, colorful genie she'd been searching for. He smiled down at her, and she smiled right back up, barely able to believe it. The adrenaline of the fight sapped out of her muscles, and she suddenly realized how weak she still was, and had to use the spear to keep standing.

"Are you okay?" she asked, not sure what was even happening.

He nodded. "Not just okay. I understand it *all* now, Lena. And it's mine again!"

"What's yours?" Coni asked, looking confused. "The shadow?"

"Nope," Jin said, grinning even wider. "My magic. *All* of it. I'm *free*! Though I do have one last wish I want to fulfill." He waved a hand, and an odd blue smoke puffed up around Lena. "There. Now you can never be hurt, not by *anything*. That one was for Sir Thomas's final wish, but I probably would have done it anyway." He slowly floated down toward them, then hugged Lena tightly as he landed. "I heard you say you're ready to write a new story, Lena," he said as he pulled away. "Me too. No more trials, no more fairy queens, no more shadow. Now, how about we put an end to all of this, then?"

CHAPTER 32

Y ou missed my whole rebellion!" a correctly sized
tiny Shefin said, crossing his arms in annoyance
after Jin and the others found him being carried on
the shoulders of a bunch of formerly human farmers, now half-
transformed back into their animal forms. "They're going to
make me their leader, and I will *rule with an iron—*"

"Nope," Lena said, grabbing him from one of the farmers
and putting him back on her shoulder. Jin had also removed the
blue dome, considering the shadow wasn't around to be much
of a threat any longer, so Shefin had quickly shrunk back to his
normal size too, and the collar-less Rufus was also back to his
normal size, now enjoying treats from a few of the farmers. "No
ruling with an iron fist. We've got things to do, remember?"

"Oh, *fine*," Shefin said, rolling his eyes. "But I think I should get a lot of credit for all this. I led the rebels to overthrow their horrible dictators! And now the bosses are going to work in the fields too!" He grinned evilly. "It was that, or I handed them over to the wolf sisters. And considering they're turning back into pigs now, I'm pretty sure they made the right call."

Susi's eyes lit up, and Coni smacked the back of her head. "Nope to you, too! We're not staying around either."

"But we can't go with them," Tala pointed out. "I don't know about you, but *I'm* not disobeying father. We still have another whole season or two in the shadowlands!"

"Not that there's much shadow left," Coni said with a shrug. "But you're right. I say we go visit that little goblin town. Lena says they can use some help."

"They've been lied to, badly," Lena said, shaking her head, having filled Coni in on what she'd learned about the goblins. "It's going to take some work to bring them around. Work, and a lot of trust."

"We've got the time," Susi said, then let out a huge howl, which sent several half-animal farmers backing away nervously. "But since we're not allowed to eat the pigs, can we at least tear down their horrible brick house?"

Coni laughed. "I feel like Father would want us to, if nothing else. He always hated pigs."

And with that, the three wolf sisters strode over to the farm bosses' house and began tearing it down with their bare hands, howling with glee the entire time. The other farmers cheered and dug in as well, enjoying the small bit of revenge.

"How did you do all of this, anyway?" Shefin asked Jin, *finally* getting to the important stuff.

"Ah, well," Jin said modestly, knowing there was no reason to brag, since his amazingness was now fully evident to everyone, but still tempted. "For the longest time, I thought I was confined to a little ring, and made to answer wishes for any master who had the ring in their possession. The only way out was to serve for one thousand and fifty years, or commit a selfless act."

"Oh, and you almost died raising my voice!" Shefin said, then bowed. "I thank you for that, as it enabled me to save the day. So that one selfless act freed you?"

Jin furrowed his brow. "I mean, first, I don't think it counts as something truly selfless since I couldn't even think straight. Plus, Lena asked me to do it, so it wasn't even my idea. And second, *you* didn't save the day. *I* did."

"You definitely helped," Shefin said, waving a hand. "That business with taking down the dome and getting rid of the shadow magic? Brilliant. But in all honesty, *I*—"

"I didn't 'get rid' of the shadow magic," Jin said, glaring at him. "I took it in, absorbed it. It's all in here." He tapped his chest.

"So now you're using its power?" Shefin asked, then gave Lena a worried look. "Are you sure he hasn't gone evil?" he whispered behind one hand.

"Shadow magic isn't evil," Lena told him, shaking her head. "Turns out it's just another genie who's been trapped for centuries. It's been used for horrible purposes, but it was always only magic, just a different kind of magic than the fairy queens liked. So they built it up as this horrible, evil shadow, and we all fell for it."

"All the genie wanted was to be free," Jin added. "Plus a little revenge against the ones who locked him away, but that's only natural. So, we're going to free him!"

Shefin gasped. "Free the shadow magic? Do you have any idea what it's done to my people? We've been living under its spell for as long as I can remember!"

"That was the fault of the Golden King, not the genie itself,"

Jin told him. "It never had any choice in the matter. Much like me, it was locked away in a certain object and controlled by whoever held that object, at least until the Wicked Queen got ahold of it decades ago. She decided to use her magic to modify the genie's prison so that her enemies couldn't use it against her."

"But that doesn't make sense," Shefin said. "The Golden King got ahold of the power somehow. How could he do that if the Wicked Queen modified it?"

"That's where the little kids come in," Jin said with a smile. "The Wicked Queen's spell made it so anyone with her bloodline could make use of the magic." He paused, considering this. "I think she wanted her granddaughter to take over for her, but instead, it just meant May and Jack's son and daughter could be used to gain control of the shadow instead, which is just what the Golden King did."

"That's right!" Jill shouted from Jin's side, a spot she hadn't left since he'd been able to understand her again, once his magic returned. "And they need rescuing already!"

"We're about to go do that," Jin told her. "Don't worry. I've got this."

"I hope so," Jill said, not looking as confident as Jin felt.

But then again, Jin now knew basically everything, *and* had his full magic as well. What in this world could stop them now?

"I'm still confused by how you're doing all of *this*," Shefin said, waving at Jin and the now sun-drenched forest beyond him. "If you didn't do something selfless . . ."

"Because I realized the truth," Jin said, grinning now. "Everything about serving a master for one thousand and fifty years, or becoming humble? Those rules weren't put into place by the elder djinn, the ifrits. They'd been imposed on me by the *fairy queens*, the only ones powerful enough to do it."

"The fairy queens?" Shefin said, looking confused. "But why?"

"Because chaos magic messes up their stories," Lena said, her face darkening for a moment. "They told me as much when I first met them, but I didn't make the connection. Chaos changes things, upsets their prophecies, so they're no longer in control."

"It all comes down to their stories," Jin agreed. "For thousands of years, the fairy queens ruled this world of humans, doing whatever they wanted. But when a genie first discovered this dimension, the fairy queens realized djinn magic was just as powerful as theirs, if not more so, and panicked that they'd lose control of the world."

"Wait, they were ruling us?" Lena said, her eyes widening. "I didn't know *that* part."

"They're not really going to just tell you that," Jin said with a laugh. "Doesn't really make them look good, you know? Anyway, the fairy queens set about tricking the ifrit who discovered this place, Marid, and imprisoned him. Only his magic was too powerful, and kept getting free. And considering genie magic is *chaos* magic, and by its nature can't help but change things, it soon started affecting the fairy queens' perfect little world."

"This is when giants and everyone were made?" Lena asked, and Jin nodded.

"And they *hate* that. They liked ruling humans, the closest creatures to the fairy queens themselves. They saw humans as little pets, basically, from what I understand. But then genie magic went and changed those pets in new, fun ways. And each of these new species had enough chaos magic inside them to really mess with the fairy queens' magic. So they had to take a different path if they wanted to regain control, and take back their world."

"Stories," Lena said.

"Exactly!" Jin shouted. "Stories about how genie magic was *shadow* magic, and therefore evil. Stories about heroic humans killing monsters like goblins and giants. Stories where slowly but surely, shadow magic would be wiped out by the fairy queens' handpicked humans. All in an effort to rule once more."

"I'm just going to say it," Shefin declared. "The fairy queens don't sound all that nice. I'm sorry, but I stand by my harsh words."

Jin laughed. "I mean, think about what they put even their chosen heroes through. All this heartache and pain for no other reason than the fairy queens wanted to be in charge." He shrugged. "Writers are always the true villains of their stories. Anyway, the more stories the fairy queens wrote to take back control, the more Marid's magic caused chaos. And they had enough trouble with just him without another genie showing up, so—"

"So they used their magic to make you believe you had to serve humans?" Lena asked.

"Exactly!" Jin said. "That's what all the stuff about selflessness was about. They wanted to be sure I was kept in line, trying to serve humans and be humble."

"Little did they know it was impossible for you to be humble," Jill pointed out.

"Anyway, it wouldn't have mattered even if I had been selfless," Jin finished, glaring at her. "They were never going to let me have all my power."

"But you do now?" Shefin said. "How did you break their control?"

"All it took was realizing what had happened," Jin said. "They couldn't actually take my power away, not chaos magic. All they could do was make me *think* I didn't have access to it. Once I realized what had happened, I just needed a bit of help from Marid to erase their brainwashing magic, and here we are."

"How did you realize all this, anyway?" Jill asked.

"Oh, it was easy, actually," Jin said smugly. "Merriweather's spell released my inhibitions to get me to tell the truth. But in doing so, it also released my access to my cosmic knowledge. But fairy magic and genie magic are very different. So if the fairies could affect my knowledge that way, it stood to reason that maybe that was because they'd imposed those restraints on me in the first place."

Lena and Shefin just blinked at this, having not heard Jill's question, but Jin didn't have time to explain. "Anyway, it's about time to fix all of this, don't you think? I don't know about you, but I'm definitely ready to do exactly what the fairy queens warned me *not* to do: open the Prison of Light, and release the rest of Marid that's still trapped within."

Shefin shook his head. "So you're going to do exactly the thing we've been trying to keep from happening, then? Unleash shadow magic on the world?"

"I'm going to unleash a trapped *sentient being* into the world," Jin corrected. "One who's been unjustly imprisoned for far too long. Plus, if we offer Marid a choice of going back home to the djinn dimension over getting revenge, I already know which he'll pick." Probably revenge, but Jin would just be more encouraging of the former, and it'd all work out.

Shefin sighed. "I don't know about any of this, but you did get rid of the sha—of the genie's magic in the shadowlands, so I guess I'm willing to go along with it."

"Good, because I wasn't really giving you a choice!" Jin said, and snapped his fingers, teleporting them all to the edge of a doll-sized city, beyond which a human-sized castle rose high in the sky, leaving the smaller city in permanent, natural shadow. "We're done following the fairy queens' plot. This is our story now, not theirs. Welcome to Lilliput."

CHAPTER 33

Lilliput was *beautiful,* as far as Lena was concerned. Everything was so small and perfect, just like the Cursed City, only in miniature. The city extended almost a hundred yards away, with the enormous castle of the Golden King blocking out most of the light from the sun giant above.

And atop that castle was the largest crystal Lena had ever seen, filled with swirling dark magic.

"That's where the Golden King has been collecting all the shadow magic he could steal from people," Jin said, nodding at the crystal. "Remember how the Faceless's swords took my magic away, and left you feeling weak? They were absorbing our magic to strengthen Marid." He grinned at Lena. "Feel like smashing that thing?"

She laughed. "I'd love to. But first, we have to find Sir

Thomas. And, uh, stop Rufus from eating anyone too, probably." She launched her arms out to encircle Rufus's neck before he could hunt down any of the tiny Lilliputians below.

Not that the Lilliputians seemed happy to see them. Between Jin, Rufus, and herself, the townspeople quickly began panicking at the sight of "giants." Little screams drifted up from below, which immediately put an end to Lena's good mood.

"It's okay!" she shouted as the Lilliputians ran from her in fear, and Rufus tried to follow them. "We're not going to hurt you! We're here to *free* you!"

"That's right!" Jin shouted, still grinning as he tromped into the now-emptying city streets. "We won't hurt you!" He threw a look back at Lena. "But how fun is *this*? Being a giant is great!"

Lena rolled her eyes. "Stop it, no tromping! Walk like a normal person. Or better yet, float us. We don't want to scare them! I've had enough people afraid of me for a *lifetime*. And *you*," she said, turning to Rufus, who hadn't stopped struggling to get out of her grasp. "No eating *anything or anyone*, got it?"

Rufus's face fell at this. "No eating," he said sadly. "But maybe later—"

"Nope!" She scratched him behind his ears to make it a little better. "These are friends. We don't eat friends."

"I'm glad to hear you say that," said a familiar voice from below, and Lena looked down to find Thomas out of his armor, surrounded by a host of Lilliputians all holding needles like the one Shefin had stabbed Jin with. "But right now, you're making a huge mistake, Lena! The Golden King knows you're here, and his Faceless will be on their way in moments. How could you disobey my orders like this?"

Jin leaned down to face Thomas, ignoring the shouted threats from the knight's rebel supporters. "Oh, don't worry, my good little man. We've *got* this. Want to come along?"

"Come along?" the Last Knight said, looking confused. "You mean to the castle? That's madness. If you're captured, all of this will be for nothing! None of us could stop you if the shadow takes you over!"

Jin just winked. "Trust me. And I know why you wanted to use the shadow magic now. I get it. It would be the only thing powerful enough to stop the fairy queens and free the world from their control. But I get why you didn't tell us. The fairy queens were watching you, and already didn't trust you. Why else would they send Lena to interfere?"

Thomas's eyes widened, almost too tiny to see. "How did you . . . What did—"

Jin picked Thomas up to look him in the eye. "We'll fill you in soon enough," he said. "But don't worry, I've got everything in hand. Literally in your case." He quickly set Thomas on his shoulder, just like Shefin on Lena's. "I'll make sure the fairy queens never push their stories on any of us ever again. Oh, and by the way, I fulfilled all your wishes, so I'm free now." He put a hand out below Thomas, who stared at it in confusion. "Ring, please?"

"Oh, I . . . right," Thomas said, and shimmied the ring off from around his waist, where he'd been wearing it like a belt. "But I still don't understand—"

"And you won't need to," Jin said, pocketing the ring. He nodded across the city. "Hey, it's our welcoming committee. Time to say hello!"

Lena glanced up to find six or seven dozen Faceless marching toward them from the castle, their magic-absorbing swords held at the ready. For a moment, she worried about what the Golden King's knights could do to Jin, considering how weak one hit by a sword had made him back when they'd first met.

But instead of fighting or facing down the Faceless, Jin just held his hands up in surrender as they approached. "You did it—we're captured!" he shouted, making the Faceless pause, surprised. "Take us to the Golden King, if you don't mind. He'll want to rant and rave in front of his enemies, if I know him. And I do."

"Are you *sure*?" Lena whispered to him. "About all of this?"

"Yeah, we're risking *everything* here," Shefin said

The Lilliputian's voice seemed to surprise Thomas, which made sense: Shefin wasn't that easy to see, tucked onto Lena's shoulder. "Shefin?" the Last Knight said. "You can't be here! I left you in safety—"

"I know, Thomas," Shefin said, sounding much less confident. "But I proved myself! I started my *own* rebellion and overthrew some horrible dictators. I can help!"

"He was pretty amazing," Lena confirmed to Thomas. "Now stop leaving people behind when all they want to do is *help* you!"

Thomas just looked at her helplessly as the Faceless neared, their weapons pointing right at Lena and her friends. Jin stepped out in front, his hands still in the air. "Well? We're your prisoners. We surrender. Let's get a move on, okay?"

"Hand over all your weapons," the lead Faceless demanded in that creepy, echoing voice of theirs. Lena knew it was just all the Lilliputians inside the armor talking at once, but it was still an eerie sound. "And submit to magic absorption by our swords."

"We just did," Jin said, and snapped his fingers. A puff of smoke appeared out of every Faceless helmet, and the lead one nodded.

"Yes, you did," it said, and motioned for a small group of Faceless to encircle them. "Now that you are helpless, we will take you to the king."

Thomas's mouth dropped open. "Did you use your magic to *brainwash* them? I didn't know you could do that!"

Jin winked at him, which made Lena shake her head fondly. With Jin's newfound power, she was actually starting to feel hopeful about all of this. In a few moments, they'd smash the Golden King's crystal containing all the magic he'd stolen using the Faceless's swords, then find the Prison of Light, and then destroy it, freeing Marid. Finally, the shadow would be gone, and the fairy queens would answer for all that they'd done.

It felt so odd to feel optimistic after all this time and everything she'd been through. But really, with Jin fully free and in control of all his magic now, what could actually stop them at this point?

CHAPTER 34

It didn't take long for the Faceless to march Jin, Lena, Rufus, and Shefin to the Golden King's throne room in this second castle. Thomas had asked to be left behind in case all of Jin's plans fell through, which Jin had agreed to, even if he knew it didn't particularly matter. At this point, the only thing he was unsure about was how long this was all going to take.

Half of him didn't want to wait even the short time the Faceless took to escort them into the castle. It would have gone much faster if Jin had just teleported them all.

But that would have ruined the surprise, and Jin couldn't *wait* to see the Golden King's face.

"*You?!*" the Golden King shouted as they entered the throne room, which looked almost exactly like the one in Midas's regular castle, back outside the shadowlands. At least, that was as far as Jin could tell after a cursory glance, considering the amount of shining gold everywhere. The king leapt to his feet and came storming down the stairs from his golden chair. "My genie, and that horrible strong girl? You've both surrendered?"

"Obviously!" Jin said, spreading his arms wide and bowing. "We're no match for you, Your Majesty. All that's left to do is admit how superior you are, and beg for mercy."

The Golden King's eyes narrowed, and he aimed his golden glove out toward them. "Do you believe me so easily fooled, genie? I have no idea what you're up to, but it won't matter once I turn you into statues. You've already lost anyway. Even as we speak, my shadow magic is covering the land, and should reach the Cursed City you love so much in a matter of hours." He grinned now, pretty evilly in fact.

Jin just shrugged. "Hey, when you're right, you're right. And you're the most right at the moment, great king, so here we are, surrendering because we lost. Here, let me help with the whole statue thing." He stepped forward and held out his hand, then shook the Golden King's magical gloved hand like they were old friends. "Hello!"

But instead of turning Jin to gold, the glove let out a puff of smoke, and the Golden King looked down in horror as a golden sheen began to spread up *his* arm. He shrieked in surprise and terror and pulled off the glove, but it made no difference now: Jin's magic had reversed the glove's power and turned its magic *inward*.

"Let's see how much you really love gold," Jin said to the king, who crashed to the floor under the weight of his golden arms, the magic spreading to his torso and legs.

"You cannot do this to me!" Midas shouted as he tried to crawl back to his throne, even as the golden magic passed his neck and reached his face. "It's not *fair*—"

And then the Golden King went silent, leaving behind a prone statue of gold, one hand raised toward his throne.

"Ah, I love symbolism," Jin said, turning back around to Lena with a huge grin. "See how easy this all is when I'm at full power?"

But Lena looked like she might be sick. "Okay, but you didn't have to do *that* to him. Can't we just throw him in jail or something?"

Jin snorted. "Jill, how do *you* feel about that, after everything he did to your family?"

But Jill didn't respond, and Jin glanced around curiously before realizing what had just happened. Of course. He'd reversed the golden glove's magic, so back in the king's original castle, Jill had just been freed from being a golden statue herself, along with her brother, sister-in-law, and their friends.

Which reminded Jin that there was something else to take care of before freeing Marid. "Lena, would you mind smashing that crystal like we talked about?" he said.

She nodded, but before he could move, she reached into her pocket and pulled out a page of what looked like ancient paper. "Just one last thing," she said, and crumpled it up with a smile. "Goodbye, *Tales of All Things*. You were the worst story I've ever heard, and I can't wait to start rewriting you."

Jin grinned, then teleported her to the top of the castle before turning his attention back to the throne. "And you two can come out now, if you don't mind."

A young boy and girl emerged from behind the throne, dark magic swirling in their eyes. "What have you done to the king?" the boy asked.

"Are you our new king?" the girl asked. "Do we have to do what you say too?"

"No, that's okay," Jin said quickly, throwing up his hands like he was surrendering. "Let's free you two of Marid's influence, okay?"

And with that, he used his outstretched hands to pull the ifrit's power out of the children. As he absorbed it into his own body, a huge crack sounded from above, where he'd just sent Lena, and another surge of power filled him, far larger than what had been contained in the twins. Jin's eyes widened at the feeling.

The Golden King had really accumulated far more shadow magic than they'd thought! This much power could have *easily* swept over the lands, putting the entire world under his control.

And now, it was all *Jin's*. He almost laughed maniacally but managed to hold it back, since Marid wasn't free yet, not to mention he didn't want to scare the twins any more than they already were.

"Where are we, Jacklyn?" the boy said, looking around like he might cry. Apparently Marid had been so fully in control that he didn't remember anything that had happened. "Where are Mom and Dad?"

"Shh, Eudoran," the girl said, hugging her brother. "It'll be okay. Mom and Dad will find us, wherever we are."

"Or you can find *them*!" Jin said, spreading his arms in what he hoped was a friendly way. "Because I'm going to send you to them. Trust me, they're going to be *very* happy to see you."

And with that, the twins disappeared in a burst of smoke, returned to their parents and their aunt Jill.

And that left just one last thing to do.

With Shefin still on Lena's shoulder, only Jin and Rufus remained in the room. He gave the enormous, annoying cat a little scratch on the head, then reached out with his senses, looking for the Prison of Light that the fairy queens had told him he must not open. Of course, they wanted to imprison Marid's magic forever, and Jin wasn't about to let *that* happen. So as soon as he located it, he'd do exactly what the fairies did *not* want him to do and *open* it.

And then Marid would finally be freed for good.

Unsurprisingly, the Prison of Light wasn't far. In fact, it was sitting right behind the throne where the twins had been, which made sense, as Jin realized they'd need to have access to it to control the djinn's magic. He waved a hand, and the Prison of Light appeared in the air just in front of him, floating at chest level.

And wow, was it not what he expected. A prison that could hold a genie should have been elaborate, spell upon magic spell forming some kind of labyrinth with no end, trapping the creature inside forever, not this . . . what was it, anyway? He considered it for a moment before the answer came to him, and when it did, he couldn't help but shake his head. A lamp, of all things? An elaborate, curved, fancy-looking oil lamp?

Without his knowledge, he wasn't sure he would have even known that was what it was. He'd certainly not seen anything like it in his own travels, but maybe that was on him. He could definitely get around more now that he was *free*. Something he'd read earlier came back to him as he considered the lamp: Merriweather had mentioned something, back in the *Half Upon a Time* Story Book, about a lamp, right before she fought Jin's ifrit parent. She'd specifically said they'd locked away an ifrit powerful enough to destroy the world in some lamp, and Jill's sister-in-law, May, had said she bet someone would find it.

"Guess you were right, person I've never met," Jin said, then reached out to free Marid.

As soon as his fingers touched the golden metal, he knew something was wrong. But by then, it was already too late.

"Lena!" he shouted, suddenly filled with terror as the lamp pulled him and every last bit of his magic inside. A moment later he was gone, and the lamp clattered to the floor, as Rufus looked around in shock. A strange sort of humming spread through the throne room, and the crumpled up page from *The Tales of All Things* uncrumpled itself, spreading out wide. As Rufus watched, now hiding behind the throne, eleven women appeared, all glowing with a strange light.

"Ah," said one dressed in blue. She reached down to pick up the golden object Jin had held, then smiled. "After my accidental interference in the story, I thought maybe your chaotic magic might ruin everything. But no, the story ended just as we intended it to, little djinn, with you trapped along with the other ifrit who caused us no end of trouble." She nodded at her companions, who moved to surround her and the lamp. "And now, finally, we can complete a task that's been waiting for millennia: the removal of *all* shadow magic from the world."

CHAPTER 35

Lena stood atop the Golden King's Lilliputian castle as broken shards of crystal fell harmlessly into its surrounding moat, and let out the biggest sigh of relief ever. "It's over," she said to Shefin, who didn't look like he quite believed it yet.

"I'm still worried about unleashing this ifrit person," the Lilliputian said, rubbing his hands nervously. "Are we absolutely sure he won't just destroy everything? I mean, if I'd been locked up that long, I probably would."

"Yes, but you also want to rule everything with an iron fist," Lena pointed out. "Let's hope this ifrit is more forgiving."

"We wouldn't have to find out if we just . . . left him in there," Shefin said, wincing a bit at his own words. "I'm not saying it'd be right, but it'd definitely be safer."

"For now, maybe," Lena said, rolling her eyes. "But what happens when another Golden King comes along, or the next Wicked Queen? They'll unleash his power under their control, and we'll be right back where we started. No, Jin's right. We have to let him out, and hope that Jin can convince him to go back to wherever they're from."

"There's a lot riding on that 'hope' of yours," Shefin said, shaking his head. "But maybe there's—"

Suddenly Lena collapsed to the roof, all of her strength disappearing out of nowhere. She dropped Shefin as she fell, and the Lilliputian hit the roof just a few feet away, then began to slide down toward the edge of the castle, yelling in terror the entire time.

"Shefin!" Lena shouted, and threw herself toward him. She managed to grab his hand in hers just before he went flying off the roof and held him as tightly as she could, though her arms felt just as weak as her legs did.

"Um, what just happened?" Shefin asked, looking as panicked as Lena felt. "And why am I . . . *growing* again?"

Lena's mouth dropped open, and she immediately tried a quick punch to the stone roof but only succeeded in sending a bolt of pain through her hand. She'd lost her strength again!

But how could that have happened? Had Marid taken back all of his magic? She couldn't blame him if he had, but that would mean such dire things for the entire world.

"Jin?" she shouted, hoping the genie could hear her. "We need help! Please, teleport us back inside!"

"I don't think he's listening!" Shefin shouted from below. "And I seem to be slipping here!"

Lena gritted her teeth, shook her pained hand, then lowered it toward Shefin. But as she moved, her weight shifted, and a stone broke away beneath her. She let out a surprised yelp as she went sliding down the roof, straight toward the now-shrieking Lilliputian.

She collided with Shefin, and they both went soaring into the air above the moat, screaming with all their might. As they fell, time seemed to slow down, and Lena briefly wondered if this was how it all ended. It would just be so ridiculous if a giant from the clouds ended up losing their life due to such a short fall, but there wasn't much she could do to stop it. The ground came flying up at her, and she tucked Shefin in her arms, then closed her eyes, letting out one last scream—

Only to slam into the cold tile floor of the Golden King's throne room, with Shefin appearing just beside her.

"You waited long enough!" Lena shouted at Jin, and tried pushing to her feet. But before she could, her entire body froze in fright as she saw who it was that had actually saved her.

"I apologize for the wait, my dear," said the fairy queen in blue, with the others smiling behind her. "I meant no harm by it. We owe you so much, don't we? True, you failed every trial, but we can't hold that against you, not when you were tainted by the shadow as you were."

"Where's Jin?" Lena said, her heart racing. The genie was nowhere to be seen now, and one of the fairy queens was holding a very unhappy Rufus, who had reverted to the size of a regular cat again. Outside she could hear screams from the Lilliputians, probably shocked at their rapid growth, if Shefin's increasing height was any indication. "What did you *do* to him?"

"We did what you were supposed to do," the fairy queen in purple said.

"We locked away the shadow, *forever*," said the fairy queen in red.

"And your friend inside with it," said a grinning fairy queen in white.

NO. How could this have happened? Jin was too powerful; he had *all* of his magic! There was no way they could have imprisoned him, too! "You're lying!" Lena shouted, balling her hands into fists, preparing to fight the fairy queens if she had to. "You never could have beaten Jin, not with all his magic back!"

"Oh, but we didn't *have* to defeat him," the fairy queen in blue said. "Because this was all a trap, young giant. The moment he touched the lamp, it absorbed his entire being into it, just as it did the ifrit all those years ago. And with the lamp back under our control, we have righted a wrong thousands of years in the making. This world will finally be rid of chaos magic, *forever*!"

"And you can become human, as you were always meant to be," said the fairy queen in purple.

"No!" Lena shouted, and ran straight at the fairy queens, not even sure what she could do. Shefin grabbed her from behind before she made it far, though, and managed to slow her down with just his still-growing two-foot-tall body, given how weak she felt.

"You can't fight them!" he hissed, shaking his head. "They're far too powerful!"

But Lena pushed him off her and stumbled toward the fairy queens again. She couldn't just let this happen—she *couldn't*! Not only was she losing Jin, but the fairy queens were going to change who she was, take away her giantness, her *magic*. And not just Lena's, but her family's, the other giants', the Lilliputians', the wolf sisters', *everyone* who'd been touched by chaos magic!

"Please, *don't do this*!" she pleaded. But the fairy queens merely began to hum, ignoring her. Not knowing what else to do, she leapt straight at the one in blue, but froze in midair as the fairy queen whistled and pointed at her.

"Now, now, let's not be upset," the blue-gowned fairy queen said. "After all, you managed to end the story exactly as we wanted, so you deserve a reward. If I remember correctly, you had a wish you wanted granted, did you not? For giants and humans to live in harmony?" The fairy queen smiled. "Consider your wish granted, child. For humans will never again fear giants, or ogres, or goblins, or anything different from themselves . . . because those things will no longer exist."

Lena opened her mouth to scream, to shout, *anything*, but it was too late, the fairy queens' music overwhelmed her, and everything faded away, the Golden King's castle immediately replaced by the Cursed City around her. . . .

Only it wouldn't be the Cursed City, not anymore. Because all the residents had been magically returned to the city by the fairy queens and were already turning human again, now no longer cursed by magic. Lil the chicken was losing her feathers, and Mr. Ralph's human form was breaking through his cookie exterior. Even Pinocchio's wooden puppet body was rapidly transforming into that of a real boy's.

"This isn't *right*!" Lena shouted at the sky, not sure what else to do as the residents of the Cursed City began panicking as well. "Please, put everything back, we can't—"

The slightest hint of a melody wafted over the wind and into her ears, and Lena's worries and fears all faded away, replaced by a warm feeling of pure happiness. All around her, the cries of shock were replaced by those of joy as the music hit the ears of the other residents, and many began hugging one another, now that their horrible curses were gone. Lena smiled at each and every human she saw now, just thrilled to be witnessing such a happy event, as tears ran down her face.

"Lena!" Shefin shouted, and Lena whirled around to find him now fully human as well. He reached out and took her hands, looking at her in a way he never had before. "We did it. We saved the entire world from the Golden King!"

Lena hugged him close and nodded over his shoulder. "We did it. And we *deserve* this, Shefin. A good life, with those we love." She grinned at him, the boy she was meant to be with. How had she not embraced this sooner? It was all so beautiful!

"May we never have to face the darkness again," he said with a grin, hugging her just as tightly.

The fairy queens had been right about *everything*. They'd sent Lena to become a better person, and she had, if only thanks to their magic. But either way, the world had been saved, and now they were ready to live out their lives as *humans*, no longer monsters.

And maybe, just maybe, she and Shefin would get something everyone hoped for, a life of peace, and their own little happily ever after.

ADDENDUM

Gwentell threw her copy of *Tall Tales* across the library, where it slammed into one of the bookshelves and fell to the floor, its spine broken. She felt so disgusted inside, so *betrayed* by her queens and what they'd done to Lena and her friends!

But what could she do? That was the end of Lena's story, according to the fairy queens, and now they were in absolute control of the human world. Without Marid's magic to keep them from interfering, they had free rein to write all the stories they wished, with their little human puppets having no choice but to play along.

No! There had to be a way to fix everything; she *knew* there was. After all, the fairy queens didn't know that Gwentell had read Lena's book. And while she didn't have their kind of power, she did have *some* magic she could use.

Maybe it was time to write one more story for Lena. Call it *Happily Ever After*, just in case the fairy queens noticed what she was doing.

But even if Gwentell wrote that story, using the fairy queens' own method of control against them, she'd need help to actually *free* Lena and Jin. But who could . . .

"Oh, *no*," Gwentell said, slapping her palm against her forehead. "Ugh, seriously? Them? *Again?*"

But she didn't exactly have many options. There wasn't a long list of humans ready to listen to her, to help her at a moment's notice.

Plus, these humans owed her, mostly for how much they'd managed to annoy her when she was last in their world.

She sighed deeply, grabbed a blank book, wrote her title on the cover, then tucked it away in a pouch for safekeeping.

And then she teleported herself to the former palace of the Golden King, where she was going to have to talk to some of her least favorite ex-statues *ever*.

ACKNOWLEDGMENTS

See, this is why I say you can never trust writers: they never have their characters' best interests at heart. Always causing trouble, writers.

The reveal of the fairy queens as villains has been a long time coming, ever since the original Half Upon a Time series. And while *Tall Tales* might have ended on a downer, the third book will be called *Happy Ever After*, which just sounds completely optimistic and upbeat, so that should be fun—*gets handed note* Uh-oh. Hmm. Ignore what I just said.

Again, I want to thank all my readers, especially YOU because you're my favorite. And I hope you've enjoyed the first two books in the Once Upon Another Time series. Just one more to go, and if Gwentell's post-credit scene is anything to go by, we'll probably even be seeing some old favorites show up.

Don't just blame me for this horrible, horrible ending,

though. Really, it's the fault of everyone who worked on this book, and I couldn't have done it without each and every one of them. To start, my agent Michael Bourret made it so that I could ruin your days with this story to begin with, while my two editors at Aladdin, Kara Sargent and Anna Parsons, did everything in their power to make those last pages that much more heartbreaking. My publisher at Aladdin, Valerie Garfield, let this all happen, while Nadia Almahdi in marketing; Cassie Malmo and Nicole Russo in publicity; Laura DiSiena, the designer of the book; production editor Olivia Ritchie; Michelle Leo and the education/library team; Stephanie Voros and the subrights group; Christina Pecorale and the whole sales team all wanted you to cry. I'm so sorry, it was them, not me!

You shouldn't blame Vivienne To, my astounding cover artist, though, as she's completely innocent.

Well, see you in *Happily Ever After*, which, if you know me, probably won't end anything like that!

ABOUT THE AUTHOR

James Riley is the *New York Times* bestselling author of the Half Upon a Time, Story Thieves, Revenge of Magic, and Once Upon Another Time series. Contrary to what his Story Thieves biography suggests, this really is James. Note to future authors: if you pretend you're not real, you'll get lots of questions.